Go-Kart Alley

Dennis R. Van Vleet

DEDICATION

This book is dedicated to the memory of
John David Catlett II.

CONTENTS

ACKNOWLEDGMENTS

This book is not perfect. It is full of typographical and formatting errors. But, I had a story in my head that had to get out. It is also not finished. There were so many elements I forgot to add that I couldn't go back and write them all. This is why there is a TV series in the works based on the book. I've written many episodes to date and each one is chocked full of daily high speed adventures that take place somewhere between Chapter Ten and Fifteen. Stay tuned to YouTube.com/GoKartAlley for updates.

Cover art appears courtesy and through the express written consent of William W. "Bill" Campbell.

Chapter 1

Jess was the first one out of the tent. The morning air was still pretty chilly that Saturday morning in the first week of April in 1986. Jess made his way straight to the smoldering embers of the last night's fire. He tore a piece off the brown paper bag they had used to tote their junk food supply to camp, wrapped it around a stick, and stirred it into the coals. It wasn't long before he had a respectable fire going again.

He looked around at the quiet wilderness. More quiet than usual, the only sound coming from water trickling in the creek. Jess looked down the tracks as he rubbed the warm radiant heat of the fire into his chilled arms. He was almost warmed when the silence was broken by the sound of the second camper coming from the tent.

It was Jess's best friend, John David Campbell. John David moved quickly to the fire, stretching and rubbing the sleep and cold away.

"Nice fire," he said. "Could ha' used that inside the tent."

"Tell me about it, I was shivering all night," replied Jess.

The final camper crawled wearily to the fire. It was Jess's little brother, Brian. He made a seat close to the fire, folded his arms tightly, and stared zombie-like at the fire.

"You're up before the train? That must be some kind'a record," Jess taunted.

Brian merely grunted at the remark.

"It's 8:14. He's right on time. It's the train that's late," corrected John David.

The tracks had been seeing less and less traffic lately, but the 8:00 train was hardly ever late. They thought little about it as they woke up and began moving around. Jess walked up onto the railroad bridge over the creek. He sat down with his feet dangling over the edge and spat between his legs into the water below, keeping a keen eye eastward in the direction of the late 8:00 train.

Jess had just turned 12 the week before. He was only slightly taller and more muscular than average for his age. He had straight brown hair, and a slim face that looked as if it could never reveal anger. He was very well-liked, but was not what you would consider part of the "popular" crowd at school. He mostly hung out with blue-collar kids that had more in common with him. He wasn't much on playing sports or joining clubs.

John David was below, skipping rocks across a swell in the creek. He was the same age and height as Jess but was stocky. Messy brown hair atop his smiley round face made it hard not to like the kid. He lived just up the tracks inside town and had been Jess's best friend since the day we moved to Sumner.

Brian finally began to move from the fire. He was a scrawny little twerp, a couple of years behind Jess and John David. He always hung around them, because they were always into something cool. For all the heck they gave Brian, he still seemed to fit in as one of the gang. He didn't even mind so much all the constant razzing they gave him, because they had proven time and again how much they actually like having him around.

"Well, I guess it ain't coming," said Jess. The boys started packing up their stuff. The conversation around the campsite was little different than the night before. They just seemed to pick up wherever they left off. Some about girls, or people they didn't like, or whatever. They gathered everything up and headed up the tracks to the gate to our place. The sweet smell of the piney woods hung in the air.

They continued to talk as they walked along the tracks. Railroad tracks are a funny thing to walk on. The crossties are spaced so that they are too close together to take them one at a time comfortably, and too far apart to stride two at a time. So they would push on alternating between two at a time, one at a time, or balancing on the rails.

We have a large acreage--almost all woods. It borders the tracks to the north, Highway 5 to the south, Sumner Creek to the east, and houses on the outskirts of Sumner to the west. The house sits two-thirds of the way in, south of the tracks. The boys wound their way up the backpath to the house. As they crossed the plank bridge over the wash, they made their way up a hill and out of a clearing behind the shed. The dumped their gear off at the shed and headed for the house.

Jess peeked his head around the door into the kitchen to see his mom enjoying a cup of coffee.

"Is dad gone?," he asked quietly.

"Yes, he's at the shop. You're safe for now," she informed him.

I let them have time off to be kids, so long as they are up and out before me. Otherwise I make them come to the shop with me! They found a loophole by camping out, to avoid getting up early on their days off from school.

"I was getting worried about you guys! You must have froze to death last night!," their mother continued.

"It was that thought of getting to sleep in those extra couple hours that kept us warm. Right, guys?," Jess replied. John David nodded, as he was focusing his attention on Brian getting a box of leftover Fred's Pizza out of the fridge.

Brian placed the pizza in the microwave and began heating it. The three gathered around to devour it as soon as it was done. Fred made the best pizza around, and it was even better the next day--if it made it that long.

The boys went back outside to put away their gear after they had finished their makeshift breakfast. Once it was put away, they enjoyed the
rest of their morning before they had to come up to the shop. At around 11:30, they started heading that way.

My machine shop was on the west side of Highway 14, right where it goes under the tracks. So, the boys headed back down the backpath to the tracks. John David was going to go home, but he decided to walk with them partway into town. It's not hard to know why. A few blocks east of the highway, right off the tracks, is where Fred's Pizza was. The boys were planning a stop on their way to the shop.

It was about a mile down the tracks to town. Coming out of the woods, they first came upon a row of houses with backyards fenced in up to the railroad right-of-way. On the other side of the houses was a vacant lot, followed by a small junkyard. Harvey Zernicke, a retired blacksmith, owned the junkyard. It was grown up with weeds and was full of neat stuff. Through the tattered fence they could see old lawn mowers, assorted piles of metal, farm equipment, metalworking machines and many other mechanical devices.

Harvey could be seen every now and then, wandering through the junk with his old dog, Sloppy. Not necessarily looking for anything, but just looking. He and Sloppy were sitting out under the awning of his old shop on this day. The boys gave a friendly wave as they passed. Harvey waved silently back.

Sloppy was a rough-looking old mutt. He was a good-sized dog with the build of a lab and the markings of a black and tan hound. He had been in a scrape or two and had the scars to prove it, like any respectable junkyard dog; but he wasn't mean. With his personality, any fight he had been in was for a good reason. Sloppy Joe, his full name, was getting a little older--not unlike Harvey--and didn't move around too much outside the junkyard.

They continued on to a crooked wooden fence with a gaping hole in it. Ducking through this hole, they found themselves at Fred's, where several kids they knew were already there. Fred's was a popular hangout for young people, because there was a game room in the back with air hockey, foosball, and a jukebox with modern rock music on it. The boys went in and ordered three slices of double pepperoni, and three ice-cold Sun-drops. They ate and did a little more visiting, until Jess and Brian had to hurry to make it to the shop by 1:00.

They were a few minutes late when they came into my office. I was on the phone.

"Well, we're on the tail end of the project now, and we need to secure a date to ship this thing out...Oh, about three weeks or so...Um, I don't
know. Two might be pushing it a little...No, it'll be headed west... Really? I guess it might have to be two then. Let me see what I can do. I'll call you back!"

I turned to the boys as I hung up the phone.

"You guys are late!," I said sternly with a smile on my face.

4

"This is starting to be a habit!"

"Well," Jess began promptly, "you know the fastest way to get here is to walk down the tracks, right? So, we were coming down the tracks when a train came. It stopped just before the highway, and did some switching and stuff. It looked dangerous to be around, so we decided to wait off to the side."

"Off to the side at Fred's, I'll bet!," I returned. "Nice try. There is a bridge out just west of Bay City. So, there haven't been any trains this way since yesterday. I was just talking to the rail yard foreman."

"So that's why the train didn't come through this morning. When do they think it'll be fixed?"

"Maybe never! The foreman said that with rail traffic slowing the way it has on this line, it barely pays to even keep it open. They will make the decision whether or not to close the line in two weeks!," I explained. "Anyway, I've got some work for you boys to do. It's a gravy job...you should be finished by 3:30."

The boys worked at the shop with me in the afternoons whenever they were out of school. It helped give them a work ethic, and a sense of accomplishment. I mean, what 10- and 12- year-olds wouldn't feel proud to go to school and know they had a hand in making their family's living? And they got to do it by running cool machinery.

Our machine shop did custom fabrication and design. We were also a job shop--meaning, we manufactured hundreds of like parts for other manufacturers to assemble somewhere else. Our shop, "McCormick Machine," employed 20 persons over two shifts, not counting the boys and me. We had all the latest machining and designing equipment, and could build almost anything!

The boys did a good bit of work around the shop. They could run the lathes, milling machines and drill presses. Jess did most of the machine operating, and Brian was his helper. They did a lot of valuable work for me. They were worth just as much as any of my other hands.

"These shafts need to be faced to a 5 inch length, and

rough- turned down to 1 ½-inch diameter," I said, lining out their work on the lathe. "Brian, you can run the saw. Cut them long by ¼- inch. These will be finish turned on the CNC lathe."

"OK, boss!," Brian said, as he rolled a piece of bar stock into the band saw vise. With that, both of them went to work. They finished up all the
parts called out by the quantity on the blueprint, and had the lathe all cleaned before 3:30. The shop was only open Saturdays on the weekend so we all went home to enjoy the rest of the weekend.

Chapter 2

A lot of work went on over the next two weeks. I used the boys quite a bit after school and on the weekends. We were trying to finish up a big mining equipment project the shop had been working on. I had gotten word from the rail company that they were abandoning repairs on the line through town. And the entire 75-mile line between Bay City and Pritchard would be closed in a few weeks.

We had finished building the equipment and were in the process of getting it all loaded onto a railcar to send to Prichard before the line was closed. The lines were to remain open going out of Pritchard so there was no danger of the equipment not reaching its final destination.

Jess and Brian were a big help in getting the equipment loaded up. They did a little of everything, from fetching supplies to driving forklift. I even found an opportunity to teach them how to weld on some braces we needed to secure some of the disassembled parts. Both boys were naturals at it.

As the locomotive coupled to the two flatcars, and one boxcar in preparation for the last haul on that line, Brian spoke. "It sure is gonna be weird not having a train anymore."

He was right. I grew up near a railroad track, and it was one of the greatest sources of entertainment to us kids. The same goes for my kids. I never gave any thought as to what it would be like not to be able to hear that lonesome clickety-clack in the distance in the middle of the night.

As the train moved out, I couldn't help but feel a little sad.

The next morning I was getting ready to go to the shop and had the TV tuned to a farm-and-ranch program out of Bay City. I wasn't paying it much attention until I heard "Rails to Trails". I walked in to listen. The commentator seemed to be quite upset about the whole thing.

It appeared that an organization had formed, in various areas of the country, which reclaimed abandoned railroad tracks as hiking and biking trails. This had many landowners upset, because original agreements with the railroads stated that when no longer in use, the rail thoroughfare was to be returned to the original landowners.

Landowners, me included, were not happy about the thought of having "city folk" tromping through the countryside leaving litter and disturbing the quiet. We saw this as an avenue for thieves to sneak onto people's property and get away unseen.

The people of Pritchard and Bay City only saw it as a wholesome source of recreation through a very scenic part of the country. They saw
nothing wrong with spending thousands to take a walk for free because of course you *have* to place rest stops and park benches, pavement and map sites all throughout the countryside before you can enjoy nature.

The landowners seemed to like their country just the way it was — as country. So hearings commenced, and the two bodies butted heads, each bringing in bigger and better lawyers to try to gain control over the 75-mile stretch between the two cities.

In the end, a Judge ruled in favor of the Rails to Trails organization. The old rails would be ripped up, and a hiking and biking trail would be put in their place.

The Rails to Trails organization forbade any motor vehicles on the trail. But, although the landowners lost the fight for the rail land, they were able to retain a few rights to jurisdiction of the trail. The trail spanned Wallace, Clearwater, and Spearman Counties. Landowners of each county governed their section of the trail. Clearwater County, where Sumner was located, passed many rules in the landowners' favor. One such rule was called "The Hardship Rule." The Sumner Area Chamber of Commerce was a big proponent of this rule. Their goal in passing it was to promote young entrepreneurship. What it meant was that kids too young for regular drivers licenses could use the trail for transportation by means of small motorcycles, minibikes and go-karts, if they had a "Hardship," hardship being a specific need such as having a job to attend or a business to support. The Chambers of Commerce of Sand Flat and Shady Grove, neighboring towns to Sumner along the trail also helped greatly in passing this rule.

Now nearing the end of April, work had begun on the trail. Crews came through pulling up the rails and ties and hauling them off. Other groups, mostly volunteers from Pritchard and Bay City, were building the rest stops and adding park benches and signs. And a crew of men, hired by a wealthy volunteer group, was paving the parts of the trail which had the most scenery, tourist attractions, motels and businesses. The entire 24-mile stretch of Clearwater County fell under that category, and was all paved. The paved sections were 8 feet wide with a yellow stripe down the middle just like a highway.

The farm-and-ranch commentator was still agitated over Rails to Trails winning out over the landowners. But he seemed to be pleased that some jurisdiction was awarded back to them. He spoke highly of the hardship rule. He felt it would be a good way to let youngsters branch out and have opportunities they might not have had before.

The hardship rule was the talk of the lunch table at school. Jess, John David, and their friend Shawn were talking excitedly about it.

"Do you know how cool this is going to be?" John David exclaimed. "I'll be able to cruise my go-kart all up and down that trail!"

"You have to get a job first or start a business," Jess reminded him. "You have to register for a trail license at the Chamber of Commerce, your parents have to sign for it, and you have to show proof why you need the license."

John David responded, "I do have a business, mowing lawns."

"Don't you mean lawn?" Asked Shawn.

"Yeah, my grandparents' yard in Shady Grove. With a trail license my parents won't have to drive me anymore and I can branch out and get more customers."

Shawn cut in, "You better get some close to home first so you can make enough to buy a new go-kart. That piece of junk of yours hasn't run for more than 10 minutes at a time without breaking down!"

"Shut up," John David laughed. "That's not a bad idea though. I could maybe get a riding lawn mower to get between jobs."

"Yeah, you could use it to pull you go-kart too 'cause it ain't never gonna run!"

"You just work on your dad's farm, you don't need the license," Jess jumped in to help John David.

"It's a job, ain't it, and what about running to town to get parts for the tractors and stuff, or when we do work on other people's farms? I could be a big help to dad then," Shawn said, defending his need.

"I suppose. Now, I have a regular job, and a real need for a trail license, but no go-kart," Jess said.

Shawn, the joker, teased at Jess, "I saw you running a forklift the other day, maybe you could cruise the trail on that. I'll be sure and wave as I blow past on the General.'Yeehaw!'"

Shawn was a huge fan of the Dukes of Hazard. He had even painted his go-kart hugger orange and added a rebel flag to make it look as much like the General Lee as a go-kart could.

"How will we know it's you and not Coy or Vance?" chided John David.

Jess and John David both started laughing.

"Yeah, that show *did* get pretty when Bo and Luke left. It was never the same, even when they came back." Shawn said. "Speaking of, did you guys watch the final episode of Hardcastle and McCormick last night?

Of course they all had. With this and the exciting news about the trail, the conversation turned into a mix of go-karts and their favorite movie and TV cars that continued throughout lunch and beyond the next recess.

Chapter 3

That afternoon, when Jess and Brian got to the shop, they were in go-kart "seek and destroy" mode. They were hatching a plan all the way to the shop. Jess had filled Brian in on what he, John David, and Shawn had discussed at school. They were going to find a way for me to let them have a go-kart if it killed them. They had tried in the past, but were never successful.

I think they were late on purpose this day, to strengthen their argument that a go-kart would help them get to work on time. Second shift began working at 3:30 and the job I had set aside for them, I had already assigned to someone else. I was out back doing some cleanup work around my little junkyard.

"I had your favorite job lined out, but I had to give it away," I said as they walked up.

"Sorry Dad. We would have been here sooner but I was helping Mrs. Harmon assemble some equipment for an experiment we will be doing tomorrow in Science class. And, that walk is just so long down the trail to here. If I were 16, I would have a *license*, and I could just drive to work."

"It's OK," I said, "you can just help me work out here until second shift is well under way. Then we can go home early."

While we were cleaning up, we reorganized some metal storage racks. There were a lot of different lengths of round metal tubing.

Jess asked, "What are you going to do with all of this?"

"Just leave it here. I'll probably never use it. But, just as sure as I throw it away, I'll need it," I said. "Why, did you want to do something with it?"

"Oh…no…I was just wondering," Jess said, feeling his plan was too obvious.

We kept cleaning and working out in the back. There was a lot of junk. Mostly old equipment we had removed from manufacturing plants when we installed new equipment. I was able to salvage pieces of it from time to time. But, for the most part, it was just stuff I would never find a use for.

There was tons of power-drive equipment--all having lots V-belts and pulleys, chains and sprockets. There were also shafts, clutches, gears, and gearboxes. Some of the old equipment I picked up was stuff like wagons and buggies that had rubber tires on them.

The boys were eyeing up the whole yard, noticing things they hadn't before. What they once considered junk, was now starting to become priceless treasures.

"Boy, you could sure build some neat stuff out of some of this!," Brian said.

"What could you build out of this old junk that'd be so neat?," I asked.

"I don't know...a go-kart or something." Brian responded.

Jess quickly glared at Brian.

I could tell exactly what they were up to because I had been in on the Chamber f Commerce meetings, but I played like I didn't know. I knew all about go-karts on the trail and saw this coming.

"A go-kart! What would you want one of those for?," I asked.

"Um...if we had one...we could use it to get to work and not be late anymore. I heard they were going to allow kids to use go-karts and stuff on the trail this summer if they have jobs," Jess said, trying to salvage his dying plan.

"I doubt that. I had one when I was a kid. The darn thing never stayed running long enough to use it for anything. I didn't know anything about working on them, and my dad didn't have time to, so the thing just sat most of the time. You boys would probably be more late, because you would spend too much time trying to fix the dumb thing. And, Lord knows, I don't have time to be working on one...or two, for that matter," I told them.

The boys were discouraged but not defeated. They would just have to keep working on me. They figured if they kept at it, I would eventually cave.

After supper when we got home, they started in again. We were sitting out on the porch when Jess spoke.

"How come you couldn't fix your go-kart yourself?"

"Well, I tried a little bit. But, I had such a limited understanding of how things worked. Small engines are kind of cantankerous. You have to have everything just right, or they won't run," I explained

"How come you didn't get someone to teach you how to work on them, so everything would be just right. Like your dad or someone," Jess continued.

"Well," I said, "my dad was always pretty busy on the farm. So he didn't have time to mess with it much. And besides, he had what I will call 'a small-engine curse.' We didn't have anything on the farm powered by a small engine, because they wouldn't work around him. It didn't matter what it was. Even if we borrowed one, it could be working fine when we got it, but it would be useless after he got around it. So he didn't go around my go-kart. My brother had taken a small-engine repair class in high school, but he was too busy chasing girls to help much either."

"So you just left it sit?" Brian asked.

"Pretty much. And that is probably what would happen to yours if you got one. Because, to tell you the truth, I still don't have much of a knack for small engines. Much less, the time to mess with them."

The boys seemed pretty discouraged. But I could tell the battle for a go-kart was not over.

They kept after me all week until Friday. That's when they finally let up on me. Or should I say, I let up on them.

It was after school, and the boys came to the shop as usual. When they walked in the office, my dad was there.

"Hey, Grandpa!" Jess greeted. "What are you doing here?"

"I'm here on business. Your dad asked me to haul up some very important equipment! He said he couldn't trust anyone else with it."

"Where did you have to haul it from?" Brian asked.

"Not very far, just from my barn."

"Yeah," I said, "he's been storing this equipment for me for a while. Now I need it, because I'm going to use it for a serious project. A project that I need you boys' help on. Come on out in the shop, and I'll show you!"

We walked out to the back of the shop. Jess and Brian didn't think much of it. They were expecting to see some old industrial equipment.

They were excited, but confused, as they rounded the corner. There near the tool room was an old, rusted, orange go-kart. Hardly the project they expected to find.

"It's a go-kart," Jess said in a confused tone.

"An old go-kart," Brian added, equally confused.

"Ain't she a beauty?" I exclaimed. "This was my mine when I was 11. I loved this 'old' go-kart. It was a big part of my life, even if it didn't run very much. I used to sit on it and dream about cruising!"

At first sight it would not look like much to the boys. It was very old-looking, covered in rust and dirt. It was once painted orange, but most of the paint was gone or faded. All of the seat cushions were faded, and one was all torn up. The motor was a rusty white color and was missing some of its parts. You could tell it was not the original motor, because some ugly rusty brackets crudely mounted it on. The gas tank was removed from the motor, and mounted to a place clearly made for a different gas tank. And there were the shoddiest homemade foot pedals on the front.

The front floorpan was hanging on by only a few welds. There were faded and peeling racing stripe decals up the floorpan that matched a plastic shield on the steering shaft. The steering wheel was cracked. There were no brakes. Two wheel rims were broken, with two flat tires. And it wouldn't even roll. The most intriguing part about it was the plastic shield on the steering shaft. The shield had yellow racing stripes up it and a small picture of a soapbox derby car that said "Orange Krate" underneath.

"The Orange Krate hasn't run in a long time!" I continued. "It ran for a total of about five days in the whole time I've had it. It originally had a 3.5-horsepower Tecumseh engine on it. That didn't last very long. In only three days it was in the shop and pronounced dead. The small-engine shop talked us into buying this 8-horse Briggs & Stratton off of a snowblower. It sat for a long time before that ever got mounted on.

"I was excited when we got it. I just knew if the 3.5-horse was fast, the 8 horse would be a lot faster. I couldn't wait, so finally I didn't anymore. I took it upon myself to mount that engine. That is what probably made it take the longest.

"My old clutch didn't fit the new motor, so I had to plead dad into getting me another. We had a lot of trouble finding one. Then I screwed up the shaft when I took the old snowblower pulley off. I had to wait before that got fixed. Finally, I tried to mount it. Of course, it wouldn't fit."

I began pointing out things on the go-kart.

"First, I had to remove the mounted gas tank from the 8-horse. I set the motor in place, and realized then that the new motor was too big and would melt the plastic gas tank mounted to the go-kart.

So I took it off. I looked at the motor again, and realized that it wouldn't mount in the holes that the 3.5-horse used. I was able to mount the front two holes by using a smaller bolt on one side, but the other two hung off the back of the mounting plate here. So I made this ugly thing, that sort of worked like a clamp to hold down the back of the motor.

"The brake band was worn out when I got it. I had taken it off to get it replaced, but I lost it over the time the go-kart was sitting. So, I didn't bother to replace it. The gas pedal got broken the first time it was running, so I made these horrible looking matching pedals by bolting together pieces of a sawed-up steel fence post. The brake pedal was made with the intention of getting brakes.

"Finally, I mounted the motor's metal gas tank up here above my head. A dangerous place, but the only one I could find higher than the carburetor. Then it was ready to run.

"I fired it up, and got on. Gravel and dust went flying as I sped off across the farm. I headed down to the pasture where I figured I would have plenty of room to tear around. I didn't make it very far before the chain came off.

"The pasture was too rough, and it kept vibrating the motor until it broke the mounting plate. So, back at the barn, I made another one of these ugly brackets to secure the front of the motor, and make up for this crack in the mounting plate.

"I was back in business. It worked good for a while there. When I wanted to stop I would just turn sharp and slide sideways. Sometimes the throttle would stick, and I would have to make several attempts to get it to stop. Once it was stopped, I killed the motor by shorting the spark plug against the motor with an insulated screwdriver. It was a crude set-up, but I was having fun.

"Although it was not as fast as I had hoped, the engine was pretty powerful. It started to wear out the clutch after a while. It got to where I had to push the front of the kart into a tree, so it wouldn't run away when I started it. Then I would get on, push away from the tree, and go back to riding. That went on until the motor died again.

"I got my brother to help me take it apart, and he fixed an ignition problem. We put it back together and were trying to get it started again, but we didn't have much luck. No matter what we did, it just wouldn't start.

"We blocked it up off the ground, so it wouldn't take off if it did start.

We messed with it until it finally started. He killed the engine, and put it back on the ground. I got on, and he pulled the cord. Nothing. It was being ornery again. So, he kept fiddling with it while I stayed in the seat. He tested the ignition by letting the spark plug wire arc against the metal of the engine while he pulled.

"It had plenty of fire. So he went to work with the carburetor, figuring it was a fuel problem. He tried choking it and unchoking it. He tried adjusting the throttle linkage. Finally, he must have done something right!

"When he pulled on the cord one last time, the 8-horse screamed to life! It took off spinning out so fast I wasn't ready for it. Neither was he, because I looked back and he was dragging by the cord! I guess he fell off…I really don't know. I was busy trying to gain control of the runaway Orange Krate. The throttle was stuck wide open. I barely managed to stop it from swerving side to side and got it going straight again. I was laughing at the excitement of going so fast, faster than it had ever gone before.

"Soon, my excitement turned to concern. I was heading down a path on the farm that went through a heifer pasture. This path had a patchy old fence along one side, and a ditch full of old junk on the other. And right in the middle of it was a herd of heifers mingling about. I was going so fast I couldn't duck through any of the gaps in the fence, and I knew I'd never make it through the ditch. My only choice was to go through the herd.

"I gripped the wheel tightly and hoped for the best. Heifers went everywhere. They were jumping and bellowing and trying to get away from the speeding dust bowl coming at them. I swerved to the left to miss one, just to swerve back to the right to miss another. There was a blur of black and white spots. Finally, I saw an opening, and I went for it. I made it out of the herd just to hit a fresh cow pie about three inches high. You may notice that the front end is only about one inch high. Manure went all up my legs, covered my crotch, up my shirt, and onto my face! I would have been worried about that, but I was too busy noticing my next obstacle.

"The path ended by teeing into an oil top road. The path had two sharp, deep ditches along both sides at this point. So my choices were limited. I could either go straight, through a five-strand barbed wire fence, or I could turn onto the oil top road. I chose to go left, because right led me out to a busy highway. I was scared of either direction, because I was going so fast I feared I might flip over. But I managed to get all the way over, next to the right-hand ditch, to make the widest turn possible. I made it without flipping, but I think I was on two wheels.

"Directly, I ran upon my next obstacle. This required no thinking because there was no option. I had to cross it. It was a cattle guard. One of those things they use to keep cattle from crossing on the road. It had bars running crossways of the road, which were spaced about 8-or 9-inches apart. If I were standing still, these tires would have fallen between the bars, and the Orange Krate would be resting on its belly. But that wasn't the case. I was going so fast I made it over the cattle guard with no problem. But it was a pretty rough ride. That is part of the reason this floorpan is all loose.

"The oil top road was fenced on both sides, and there were several cattle guards along it. It ended at a pumping station where an oil company serviced oil wells. The station was full of pipes and equipment. I was doomed if I got in there. My only chance was a patch of loose gravel off to the side of the last stretch of road before the station.

"When I got to it, I gradually veered off of the road, onto the gravel. I then cranked the wheel hard to the left and hoped for the best. The Orange Krate slid sideways for a little bit, and then made its way back around, sliding backwards, but pointed in the direction from which I came with the wheels spinning and throwing gravel. I veered back onto the road, and headed back across the cattle guards.

"I wanted to kill the motor on the straightway, but I lost my screwdriver on one of the cattle guards. So Plan B was to try to get back up by the barn to where maybe my brother could help me get it stopped. I was nearing the last cattle guard before I had to make the turn back up the path to the barn. I was noticing that heifers had made their way back into the middle of the path. I was eyeballing the turn, but I hesitated because of the heifers and waited too long. I couldn't make the turn without flipping, so I missed it. I was heading straight toward the highway.

"It was coming closer and closer. I had no idea what I was going to do. As I got near the hayshed, I noticed another of those patches of loose gravel off to the side. This one was a lot smaller, and had big rocks and clumps of grass growing out of it. I feared I might hit something and flip. I was out of options. I had to try. I veered off once more and cranked the wheel. This time I was going way too fast. The Orange Krate just kept sliding sideways. The motor was roaring uncontrollably. I was sliding directly toward a wooden fence post at a high rate of speed. I just knew I was going to plow right into it and be badly injured.

"But, suddenly, the motor just died. Like someone just hit it with a hammer. The Orange Krate slid to a stop, just inches from the post. The roaring engine sound was gone. The only sound was that of gravel showering to the ground from the now stopped, spinning tires. I looked behind me to see a huge sideways tornado of dust that had spun off of the wheels in the dust.

"I just sat there for a second. When the dust cleared, my brother came running up from behind.

'Man, you were really flying!' He said. 'Why did you stop?'

"I told him I didn't, and recapped the whole story. We gave it a good looking over to assess the damages. The cord was still hanging out of the recoil, and was wrapped around the back bar. These two wheels were broken and the tires were flat, probably from sliding sideways across the rocks.

"Yes, sir, it was a pretty hairy ride!" I said, wrapping up my harrowing story.

"What did you do with it after that?" Jess asked.

"Well," I said, "I managed to fix the recoil where it would reel the cord back in. But, the mechanism that allowed it to grab the shaft was messed up. I wrapped a rope around the shaft and tried to start it that way. Even when we did get a good pull on it, the engine never showed any interest in starting. School started back, and I got busy. We put it in the barn, and it has been there ever since."

Both boys had hung on every word of the story. Images of getting the old kart going again were practically visible in the gleam in their eyes.

"So, now, you boys get to get to pick up where I left off. What do you say we finish up things around here and get to the small-engine shop before it closes? We're gonna need a lot of parts to get this baby going again!" I told them.

"So, when we get it back running again, me and Brian get to keep it?" Jess asked.

"Well, not exactly. When you get it all fixed up, I want to retire it," I replied.

"What!" Brian exclaimed.

"See, I want you to restore my old go-kart for me, and in turn you get to gain the skills to build your own. Of course, you will get to drive the Orange Krate while you are building your own. Does that sound like a good idea?" I said.

"Sure, it does!" Jess exclaimed. "We get to design and build something really cool that is all our own!"

"Right down to the drink holder! I figure if you learn how to build and rebuild a few go-karts, you will know more about them than me. Then you'll be able to fix your own when they break down. You already have more mechanical skills than when I was your age," I said. "But I still think you'll be late for work!"

Chapter 4

I picked up one end of the Orange Krate, and the boys rolled the other. We carried it out to the truck to take to the small-engine shop. I picked up an old, adjustable engine mounting plate from out back and loaded it up as well. Dad had to get going, so we said goodbye to him.

I went back in the shop to ensure everything was going well on second shift. When I was sure that it was, we headed to Sumner Small Engine.

When we pulled up, the first thing we did was get a pad and a pen to write down any serial number information off the old motor. We took that inside to give to the parts man.

The shop owner wasn't the nicest man in the world. His prices were kind of high, and he didn't act like he really cared whether he got your business or not. But, he was the only dealer in town. Jess sat the notepad on the counter.

"We need a complete overhaul kit, and both valves, for an 8-horse Briggs," I told the parts man, sliding him the pad.

He squinted down at the numbers on the pad through his bifocals, and went to looking into his parts catalogues.

The boys had found their way around the shop, looking at anything remotely related to go-karts. They were checking out the bigger and better motors on display. Then they turned their attention to what was sitting in the front window.

I was a brand new go-kart. It was shiny, candy apple red with some white pinstripes. It had polished aluminum pedals, and spoilers, front and back. It was made to look sort of like an Indy car. The motor was a brand new 5-horse Briggs & Stratton. They were pretty taken in by its newness at first.

"Whoa...I want this one!," Brian said in awe.

"No you don't. We can design something a whole lot cooler than this one. Ours will be a lot cooler. Besides, look at the price. Who could afford something like that?" Jess told his little brother.

"Here you are." The parts man said laying the rebuild kit on the counter.

I couldn't think of anything else we would need from there that we couldn't get from the auto parts store. So, I paid for the parts, and we headed home.

When we got there, we just grabbed some peanut butter and jelly sandwiches for supper. The boys were anxious to get to work on the go-kart. So, we carried our food out to the shed with us.

Mom came out to eat PBJs with us and watch for a little while. She decided it looked like we were having "Male Bonding," so she left us to go work in the garden.

We unloaded the Orange Krate and carried it into the shed. The shed was a 16 ft. by 40 ft. wooden building with concrete floor and a shingled roof. Looking at it from the house, it had two roll-up garage-type doors on the long sides--starting about 6 feet from the left end--one on each side of the building. You could go straight through if they were both open. The shed sat a good ways back diagonally behind the house and to the right a little, with the long sides facing the in the direction of the trail to the north and the house to the south. On these sides there were a few windows made of clouded glass and covered with metal bars.

Inside to the left there was a workbench along the end, with storage shelves underneath, and a bolt cabinet on top. The other end had two 8 ft. by 8 ft. storage rooms. In between the roll up doors and the storage rooms was working space containing three worktables.

The shed served as my workshop at home. It housed several tools that I had written off from the machine shop in town and brought home to use for projects around the house. They were still useful machines, but newer machines had just replaced them.

Along the north wall away from the house was an 8-inch South Bend engine lathe. Between it and the storage room was a small Bridgeport knee-type milling machine. Along the south wall closest to the house was a welding/cutting table, as well as a practically brand new MIG wire welder, accompanied by an ancient stick welder and acetylene cutting torch. Between them and the storage rooms was a large air compressor.

The machines, except for the wire welder, matched the rest of their surroundings. It was a little dark and greasy in the workshop, and everything in it looked like it had seen its share of work. The shed was used by the people we bought the house from as a place for restoring small old tractors.

We picked up the Orange Krate and set it on the first worktable. I went back and got the universal mounting plate and set it on the workbench.

"The first thing we'll do," I said, "is mount this to the work bench. We can use it to hold the motor in place while we work on it."

So I found some screws under the bench, and secure the plate in place.

"Jess, pull that rollaway toolbox over by the go-kart," I said. "You boys can use all of the tools you like. Just take care of them, and put them back when you're done."

With the tools at hand and everything in place, we went to work. I told them which wrenches to get and instructed them on how to remove the old and ugly brackets I had built. The nuts were rusted onto the bolts. But, with a little work and some WD40, they came off. There was no chain anymore, so all there was left to do was to take the gas line loose from the tank. The gas had dried out long ago, so there was no danger of spilling any. Together they carried the 8-horse over to the bench.

I adjusted the brackets on the universal plate to match the motor. Brian got the proper bolts out of the bolt cabinet to mount it down. Jess put them in place, and tightened down the motor.

"The flywheel cover with the pull cord was lost, so we'll have to see if we can find one down at Harvey's. The first thing I want to do is pull off the head," I said.

Years after the Orange Krate had quit running I was thinking about it, and I figured out what had happened to the motor that last time it ran. So I told them to go straight to the problem area.

They took a long socket wrench and loosened all of the

head-bolts on the top of the engine. Together they removed the bolts, and lifted the head off.

Underneath they were able to see the piston and the valves. From above, the piston looked like a larger circle down in a hole, and the valves were two smaller circles off to the side of the hole. One of the valves was flat with the top of the engine. The other was sticking up about ¼ inch.
I slowly turned the flywheel. The piston went up and down in the hole, and one of the valves would open and close every other time the piston came up. The other valve stayed up the whole time.

"Just as I thought!," I exclaimed. "The exhaust valve is stuck open."

I tried to push it down, but it was frozen and wouldn't budge. This was the reason the motor had died so suddenly when it did. I proceeded to explain this to the boys.

"With this valve open, the piston can't achieve compression, and the engine is allowed to freewheel!," I said.

Both of them were looking at me as if I were speaking French.

"Okay," I said, "I'll explain it to you. This is a four-stroke, internal combustion engine. What that means is that it burns fuel internally, in four distinct 'strokes' of the piston. The four strokes are: Intake, Compression, Power, and Exhaust. I'll show you by turning the flywheel. When the piston is all the way up, even with the top of the engine like this, it's called 'top dead center'. Top dead center is the start of the first stroke, the intake stroke.

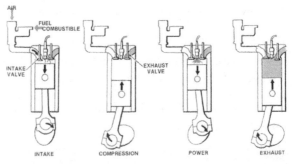

"As I turn the motor, and the piston goes down, this intake valve opens." The flat valve came up from even with the top of the engine. "When the piston is going down, it draws air into the cylinder through the intake valve. Fuel is mixed into the intake air by the carburetor here on the side of the engine. When the piston reaches 'bottom dead center', the intake valve closes. This exhaust valve is *supposed* to be closed this whole time.

"When the piston comes back up, it starts the compression stroke. With both of the valves closed, and the head in place, there is nowhere for the fuel and air to go, so the piston squeezes it tight in the top of the cylinder, kind of like pushing down on a bicycle air pump with the hose stopped up.

"The air and fuel mixture is squeezed as tight as it can get when the piston reaches top dead center again. At this point, under high compression, the fuel is most explosive.

"At top dead center, the spark plug sparks, and ignites the fuel. The fuel then basically explodes, forcing the piston back down on the power stroke. Both valves remain closed during the power stroke, so all the power of the explosion acts on the top of the piston.

"The piston comes back up one last time on the exhaust stroke. This is where the exhaust valve *is* supposed to be open. On it's way back up, the piston forces all the exhaust gases out the exhaust valve, and on out the muffler.

"At top dead center, after the exhaust stroke, the four strokes begin again--intake, compression, power, exhaust."

The boys could see it then.

"So, when the piston comes back up on the um...wait, let me think." Brian went through the motions of the piston by acting out the stroke using his fist as a piston. "The compression stroke, with the valve stuck open like it is, the gas never gets compressed?"

"That's right," I answered. "Like trying to push on that bicycle air pump with a hole in the end."

"So what do you think caused the valve to stick like that," Jess asked, "just being rusty or something?"

"I'm glad you asked. I think we'll find out if we keep taking the engine apart and look at the governor," I said.

We were going to do a complete overhaul, so we proceeded to take the entire engine apart. The next step was to remove everything from either end of the crankshaft; this included the centrifugal drive clutch, the "recoil" starting clutch, and the flywheel.

With everything free of the crankshaft, they were able to take off the crankcase cover. Once the cover was off they finally got to see some of the "guts" of an engine. It was black and oily inside. Several gears were visible, as well as the "crank" part of the crankshaft. One of the gears visible was made on the crankshaft. The other was made onto another shaft. Still another gear was visible still in the crankcase cover. I took immediate interest in that one.

It was a cup-shaped gear and had a few strange pieces mounted in the middle. In the center of the strange pieces was a pointed rod. I was paying close attention to this gear.

"This is the governor," I told them. "This is what controls the speed of the engine."

"I thought the throttle on the carburetor did that," Jess said.

"Well, it does too, sort of." I responded. "I'll explain it. What actually does the controlling of the speed of the engine is a butterfly valve up here above the carburetor. It allows, or restricts the amount of airflow into the engine. It is just a disk in a pipe, that when turned one way, closes the pipe and won't allow any air through. When it is turned the other way, exactly one-quarter turn, it is so thin that it allows maximum airflow to the engine. So, with maximum airflow, comes maximum fuel. And the engine is allowed to go as fast as air can flow through the pipe. That is too fast for the engine to hold up. This is where the governor comes in. The governor will not allow the engine to go too fast for its own good."

"Couldn't you just put in some sort of stop that wouldn't let the butterfly open all the way up?" Brian asked.

"That's the thing. Sometimes you want the butterfly to open up," I continued explaining. "When there is a loss of power, like going up a steep hill, the motor will bog down.

When the motor slows in speed, the governor responds by opening the butterfly, and giving it more gas. The motor will speed up until it reaches its previous speed, and then it will level off. It responds constantly to changes in motor speeds and reacts to keep it regular."

"Then how come you still have to push in the gas pedal when you are going up a hill?" Brian asked.

"Because the governor will only speed the engine up to its previous speed. The speed you had set with the gas pedal before. If you still need more power to get up the hill, you have to allow the governor, to allow the butterfly, to allow the engine to speed up, by pushing on the gas," I said.

They moved in as I began inspecting the governor assembly more closely. I was moving the weights of the governor in and out when I noticed something.

"Ah-ha!" I exclaimed. "Here's our culprit."

There were two weights mounted to the gear. Each pivoted on a hinge pin. These weights slung outward from the center of the gear when the engine sped up. That is what caused a cone to push against a linkage that closed the butterfly. But one of these weights had come part way off its hinge pin. The weight was crooked, and lodged to where it would not move.

"With this weight like this, the governor is useless and can not control the speed of the motor. This is why the engine was going so fast the last time it ran. It ran so fast, for so long, that the engine could not hold up. These valves were moving up and down so fast that the exhaust valve bent and stuck open," I said.

Satisfied that we had found the problem, we continued to tear down the engine. I named all the parts and explained all their functions as we went along. The next thing we had to do was to remove the valves. This required a special tool called a valve spring compressor. Once the valves were removed, we would be able to remove the camshaft. The boys removed a plate on the side of the engine at my order.

"These springs," I said, pointing under where the plate had been removed, "are what hold the valves closed. They are under compression now, so we'll have to use this tool to squeeze them together, so we can remove the keepers, and then the valves."

Jess placed one end of the tool under the spring, and tightened the screw on the other end of the tool, against the top of the valve. Brian took a pair of needle-nosed pliers and removed the keeper. Jess loosened the screw, removed the tool, and the valve came out freely. They repeated this for the second valve.

Brian overanxiously pulled on one of the gears to remove the camshaft. When he did, two small parts fell into the crankcase. He looked at me as if he had done something wrong.

"That's OK," I said. "You'll just have to be more patient. Those were the tappets. Now, take a look at this shaft. You see the egg-shaped things?"

"Yeah." Both boys responded.

"Those are called cams. They are what lift the valves on the intake and exhaust strokes. When the camshaft turns, the long end of the cam comes around, it pushes up on the valve stem that slides up and down directly above. These tappets are what actually ride along the surface of the cam and push against the valve.

"The camshaft has to turn at just the right speed so that the valves operate at the correct times. The gear on the crankshaft turns the camshaft gear. The difference in size of these gears, or the 'gear ratio' is just so that the camshaft will rotate at the proper speed, and the valves will open at the right times."

There were only a few steps left in disassembling the engine. They were to remove the piston, the connecting rods, the crankshaft, and the ignition components.

I pointed out the crank and the connecting rod. "This is where the crankshaft gets its name. This part of the shaft works just like a crank on an old-fashioned ice-cream maker, or the pedals on a bike. The connecting rod attached to the crank is also attached to the piston. That is why it is called the 'connecting' rod. It connects the piston to the crank.

"The rod acts like the lower part of your leg on a bicycle crank, and the piston is like the upper part of your leg, the source of the power.

"When you take this cap off the bottom of the rod, the piston and rod will be able to come out the top of the engine, and we can pull the crankshaft out of the crankcase."

Jess grabbed a wrench and removed the rod cap and oil slinger. He turned the crankshaft to where it pushed the rod as far up as it would go, and then it stayed there without the cap to pull it down. He then swung the rod out of the way of the crank, and removed the crankshaft. With the crankshaft out of the way, he gave a hearty push on the bottom of the rod and pushed the piston out of the top of the cylinder block.

Brian removed the ignition components, including the points and coil. Jess was taking the piston loose from the connecting rod. Brian also removed any remaining sheet metal. After the carburetor and muffler were off, they worked at completely taking everything apart, with me explaining all of the functions as they went.

When the engine was completely disassembled, we placed all of the parts into groups on the bench. We did a quick inventory to make sure we hadn't lost anything and put up all of our tools. It was getting pretty late, so we decided to call it a night. Work was slow at the shop, so I was taking the weekend off. The boys and I would continue to work on the go-kart the next day.

Chapter 5

We were up early the next morning. Breakfast was a quick bowl of cereal, because we wanted to get to work on the go-kart. I rolled up the door on the shed and flipped on the lights. We were hard at work before the sun came up.

The first thing I had the boys do was to rebuild the carburetor. The overhaul kit included a carburetor kit, so we had all the parts that could be replaced, including a new butterfly valve and gasket seals. They carefully cleaned and inspected the parts of the carburetor. They installed all the new parts and reassembled it.

The entire block, and all of the engine parts, got a good cleaning and overall inspection. Everything was in good shape except the governor. They worked hard and replaced all of the worn engine parts with new ones from the kit. The engine was almost back together except for the crankcase cover and governor. By that time it was after 8:00 am, and we headed up to Sumner Small Engine to get a new governor assembly and governor spring.

When we got back to the house we installed the new governor and closed the crankcase. The head was back on, with a brand new spark plug in it. The only thing left was the ignition parts, the flywheel, and the flywheel cover.

Brian installed the ignition parts, because it required a steady hand and patience. Jess was easily aggravated with small parts, but Brian was good with them. I showed them how to properly set the ignition timing, so that the spark plug would fire at the right time.

Jess attached the flywheel, a new recoil starting clutch and a used flywheel cover we got from Harvey's while we were in town. I inspected all of the throttle linkage and adjusted the carburetor a little. The new flywheel cover had a good starting rope and handle. It looked like we were ready to give it a try.

I took the spark plug wire and held it close to the head while giving the rope a pull. A big blue spark jumped from the wire to the head.

"Looks like we got fire!" I exclaimed. "Let's hope we have fuel. Jess, would you like to do the honors?"

I put the spark plug wire back on the spark plug. Jess grabbed the starting rope, braced himself, and pulled back as hard as he could. Amazingly, the engine roared to life on the first pull!

"Looks like the McCormick small-engine curse might be ending with you guys!" I said to the boys' who were smiling with delight at the sound of the old motor.

We let the engine run for a while. Brian adjusted the carburetor some more until the engine was running as smooth as could be. He would rev the engine with the throttle. Each time he revved it, it would return to a smooth idle.

I killed the engine by grounding the spark plug to the head with a screwdriver.

"Now that the engine works, we can get on to the frame. We'll give the engine a new coat of paint when we start painting the rest of the go-kart," I said.

We moved back over to the rusty old frame on the work table. The boys went to work taking everything apart and leaving behind only the metal frame. We began inspecting the frame for cracks and bends. The old mounting plate was going to be replaced by a new one that would fit the 8-horse. So, the cracks in it didn't matter much.

Jess got the measurements off the mounting holes in the 8-horse. There was some scrap metal out back, so we went to find a piece that would work as a new mounting plate. Jess laid out the rough shape that the plate had to be and cut it out using the acetylene torch. When it cooled, he took it over to the milling machine and machined it properly square. He then clamped it to the table and milled the adjustable mounting slots in it. He used the torch to cut off the old mounting plate and laid the new one in place.

I showed them how to set up the wire welder and let them make a few practice beads on the old mounting plate. Jess was a natural at the welder torch and metal machines, with precise and swift work habits; where it looked like Brian had more of a knack for engines and tweaking.

With Jess the better welder, he welded the new plate in place, careful to make sure it was square with the frame. He flipped the frame over and fixed all of the broken weld beads on the floor pan. There were a few bent places on the frame, so he used the torch to heat them up and bend them straight. The frame was now in good shape.

"That's about it, right? We're ready to put it back together now," Jess said.

"Not so fast there," I told him. "We have to pull all these wheels off and replace the broken rims. And we have to replace the bearings and fix the flat tires make new pedals, mount this gas tank better, add a new throttle cable, and add some brakes. Plus, there is one more modification I want to add."

They dove back into work. Jess sketched out some new pedals he thought he could build. I made a few changes to his sketch, and told him to build them that way. I also told him to make four pedals instead of two. He was puzzled, but went to work anyway.

Brian took the wheels off of the axle and spindles, and laid all of the old bearings out on the workbench. He and I set the motor on the frame and measured out the length of the throttle cable and brake cable. We made a list of things we needed for our last trip to town.

We had a late lunch and went back into town. We found new bearings up at the shop. We got a new brake band and wheel parts at the small-engine shop. We stopped in Hawkins Auto Supply last.

I walked up to the counter but there was no one attending it.

"Well boys, it looks like everything in the store is free," I said loudly. "Just start carrying stuff out to the truck!"

Carl Hawkins, the owner, came out of the parts shelves in the back of the store.

"Go on. Take it all so I can go home," he said dryly. "What do you want?"

"We're in the process of rebuilding a go-kart. We've got

almost everything done and we'll be ready to paint by this weekend. What's the fastest looking color car paint you sell?" I asked.

"Calf-poop yellow. High gloss," he responded.

"Great, give me three pints of calf-poop yellow then," I told him.

The boys looked at us in horror. Carl walked to the back and came back with three cans of paint.

"Sorry, we're all sold out. You'll have to settle for Hugger Orange," he said.

The boys breathed a sigh of relief. I had ordered the paint we needed earlier that week, so Carl knew what we were there for. He had brought up a quart of Hugger Orange, one pint of Canary Yellow, and one pint of High Heat Gloss White.

"Is that all?" He asked.

"We need some throttle cable, and an idler pulley about three inches in diameter," I told him.

I looked around the store trying to think of anything else I needed before he closed for the afternoon. As I looked, I noticed a Briggs & Stratton sign.

"You sell small-engine parts?" I asked him.

"Yeah, I switched parts distributors here a while back. I can get all parts for all makes and models of small engines," he said. "I can get just about anything except new engines."

"I'll bet Sumner Small Engine wasn't happy about that!" I said.

"He ain't happy about anything. He only likes to do business with his cronies anyway," he said.

I paid for the supplies, and we were off to the shed to go back to work on the go-kart.

Back at the shed, Brian started replacing the old wheel and axle bearings. Jess was finishing up the pedals he was building, and I was making some calculations on a notepad at the bench. When they were finished with everything I had laid out for them, they came over to where I was working.

"How should I mount these pedals?" Jess asked, walking up.

"I'll show you in a second," I said. "I have to finish this

first."

"What is that?" He asked.

"Remember those modifications I wanted to make?" I asked. "I'm calculating how to go about it. I don't want to go back with the centrifugal clutch. I want to use a different kind, and I'm making some calculations on the proper gear ratio for this engine."

They looked at my sketches.

"The old centrifugal clutch was not heavy enough for this engine. I always wanted to try a belt clutch instead," I said. "That way, you can take the go-kart out of gear, rev the engine up, pop the clutch, and spin the tires. Also, if you ever have trouble starting it, you can always let it roll downhill, and pop the clutch."

"How does a belt clutch work?," Brian asked.

"Instead of using a chain and sprockets, you use a belt and pulleys. The only thing is that you leave the belt loose. The belt must be loose enough that it won't burn on the engine pulley. You mount an idler pulley on an arm that pushes in on the loose belt to tighten it. When the idler is engaged, and the belt comes tight, the go-kart will take off. We'll use a spring to pull the idler arm tight, and a clutch pedal to release it."

"So why did you have me make four pedals? Don't we only need three?" Jess asked.

"I wanted to put the gas on the far right, the clutch on the far left, and two brake pedals in the middle," I said. "That way you can run the brakes with either foot if you have to. The two brake pedals will be linked together.

"What did you mean about the gear ratio?," Brian asked.

"I have to figure out what size pulleys to use," I said. "Just like on a 10-speed bicycle, when you have to determine which sprockets to put the chain on. You as the bicycler, only have so much speed and power. You've probably noticed that when you put the chain on a big sprocket at the pedals and a little sprocket on the wheel, it is really hard to pedal, but it goes faster. The opposite is true when you put it on a small sprocket on the pedals, and a large sprocket on the wheel. It is easy to pedal, but it goes really slow."

"I've noticed that," Jess said.

"I'm finding the proper mix in the middle, between big-small and small-big. Because this engine, like the bicycler, only has so much speed and power," I said.

I finished my calculations and got a pulley out of the truck that I had picked up from the shop. The pulley would fit on the axle, but I didn't have one for the engine. I found some suitable metal from the scrap pile and took it to the lathe.

My calculations included a sketch of the pulley I needed. I walked the boys through how to make a belt pulley. They worked hard and finished it rather quickly.

We made some measurements for the clutch and pedal mounting, and the boys went to work. It wasn't long before the clutch brackets were on and the pedals were in place.

We reviewed everything that had to be done to rebuild the kart and checked it against what we had done. It now looked like all we had to do was paint it and put it together. We took a break for supper.

After supper we were back in the shed to work. I told them we should assemble the kart and try everything out before we painted it. We wouldn't want to weld anything after painting.

The boys worked diligently assembling the go-kart. They could hardly believe how it was coming together. It wasn't long before the engine was on, and everything was assembled.

The clutch and brakes looked as if they were adjusted right. The throttle worked fine and didn't appear to stick.

We carried the Orange Krate out of the shed, and under the yard light. Jess was to first to take his seat on the rusty metal frame. He pushed in on the clutch and brake, and locked them in place with catches we made on the linkage. He got off and propped his left foot on the back bar. He grabbed the cord, and gave it a firm pull. The engine fired up. He revved it up a few times with the linkage on the carburetor.

Looking back at Brian and I with a big grin, he took the seat again. Revving the engine, he popped the clutch and spun gravel at our feet. He sped off across the yard and made a few laps in and out of obstacles in the yard under the light of the pole by the shed.

Brian took an equally long turn before returning it to the shed. He brought it into the shed with a sliding stop. Both seemed to be exhilarated by the experience.

We enjoyed a few bottles of Sun-drops while the motor cooled. The boys shared stories of what all they planned to do with their own go-karts once they built them.

When the motor had cooled, we went to work disassembling the kart again. It was back down to just a rusty, welded-up metal frame.

"The first thing we have to do before we paint is to sandblast it, to get off all the rust and old paint." I said.

I turned on the air compressor while they filled up the blaster with sand. They had used a sandblaster at the shop before, so they knew just what to do. They worked on the blasting while I cleaned out one of the storage rooms.

They finished blasting all the parts to be painted and I set up some sawhorses in the storage room. I made sure the exhaust fan was working and put a dust filter over a 12-inch-square hole in the door.

"This will serve as a paint booth and will cut down on the dust to make a better finish," I told them when they had finished carrying in all the parts.

We got out all of the painting equipment and protective gear. We mixed the paint with thinner and hardener. It wasn't long before they were painting.

By 12:30 am, the Orange Krate was orange again. We cleaned up the shed and painting equipment and called it a night. It had been a long but productive day.

We sneaked a peak at the go-kart before church the next morning, because we couldn't stand not to. After church we taped off the white-and-yellow racing stripes and painted them. Those dried while the boys reassembled the kart. By late afternoon, the Orange Krate was back to its original condition--slightly modified, of course!

Chapter 6

We were a little slow at the shop so I let the boys have the afternoons off for a week. It was shaping up to be a fine spring and it didn't seem right to keep them from enjoying it after being cooped up in a school all day. Not to mention down right cruel to keep them from riding there new, old go-kart that I was so proud of them for rebuilding. So, for the first part of the week after school, the boys enjoyed riding around the land on the Orange Krate. They took turns riding up and down the driveway in the glorious late afternoon spring sunlight. They had developed a regular racing circuit around the house and buildings. They even spent some time off the go-kart to smooth out the backpath that led from the shed down to the old railroad tracks. They wanted so badly to drive on the new trail, but it wasn't finished yet, and there were still people in Sumner working on it who wouldn't have let them.

On Wednesday, Brian was waiting by the shed when Jess came in, sliding to a stop from his turn. He killed the engine by flipping down a toggle kill switch on a piece of aluminum plate we mounted between the steering support bars near the base of the seat.

"I don't know if it's just that I'm getting better or what but it doesn't seem very fast anymore." Said jess getting of the Orange Krate.

"Yeah, I was thinking that too on my last turn. I was thinking 'I don't see how dad had so much trouble controlling it the last time he said it ran.'" Brian replied.

"But he had that governor problem, remember?"

"Yeah…wait a minute. I've gotta see something."

Brian went into the shed to get something. When he returned he was carrying some wooden blocks.

"Lift up the back end I wanna block it up."

Jess picked up the rear of the go-kart and Brian stacked the blocks under the back bumper. Jess set it back down. Brian went around to the front and switched the kill switch on, then came back, grabbed the starter cord and fired up the engine.

"Givver some gas with the pedal. All she's got." Brian told Jess loudly over the sound of the idling engine.

Jess did so with an outstretched foot and the RPMs accelerated to a level they were familiar with from riding it around all afternoon as "wide open." Brian moved his head around looking determinately at different parts of the throttle linkage. He saw where the throttle cable came in and where we had tied it to the linkage on the engine. He traced the engine linkage to the governor lever. Jess craned his neck to see what Brian was doing. Brian reached in and pushed on the end of the governor lever.

Jess's eyes widened with surprise as the engine revved slightly higher when they thought it was wide open. Brian recoiled his hand and shook his wrist as though it had been hard to push. The enging slowed to its previous level.

Looking at the engine with even more determination Brian continued to trace the linkage up to the butterfly lever on the side of the carburetor. He reached in once more and the butterfly lever with ease. The engine really revved up then. The RPMs were accelerating rapidly and the whole go-kart began to shake with a sort of wild vibration until it sounded like the engine might run away with itself and fly apart. Brian let off the butterfly and the engine slowed down to its previous level again. Brian goosed the butterfly twice more and then gave it another long rev before making a slitting motion on his neck signaling Jess to "kill it." Jess let off the gas pedal and flipped down the toggle switch near the seat.

"Wow! How'd you do that?" Jess asked as he walked around to the back of the go-kart to take a look.

"Remember when dad touched on the purpose of the governor? Well, I didn't understand it then but I think I do now. The way we've got it hooked up, we're not actually controlling the throttle, we're controlling the governor. The way it's set up now is stock from the factory. It's like they didn't want us opening it up all the way for safety or something. But the governor can."

"Like if you're going up a hill and need more power the

governor kicks in." Jess chimed in.

"Exactly. The governor responds when the RPMs drop. But that not what we want. We want full throttle, the real wide open."

"So how do we get that?"

"I'm thinkin' we just unhook the governor and tie our cable directly to the butterfly."

"Will that work do you think?"

"Only one way to find out."

And with that the two boys took the kart down off the blocks and pushed it in to the shed near the tools to make the necessary adjustments to try out Brian's idea.

On Thursday, they went to John David's after school. After hearing all about how they rebuilt a go-kart engine themselves, John David wanted them to stop by and look at his go-kart. He had a problem with it cutting out all the time for no apparent reason.

The boys were anxious to help out. John David opened up his garage to get to the go-kart. His kart was faded red and built kind of blocky. It had a white seat with a black lightning bolt on it. It was powered by a 3-horse Briggs and Stratton.

"It takes forever to start, and then it never stays running." John David said.

He grabbed hold of the cord and tried to start it. It took three or four tries, but it started.

"Probably gonna make a liar out of me. It's usually harder to start than that," he shouted over the engine. "Drive it around and see what you think."

Jess got on and drove John David's go-kart out of the garage, around the corner, and down the alley behind the houses. He rode down a short way and turned to come back. On the way back, he pounded through some dried ruts in the dirt path. Halfway back, the engine began cutting out, and then died.

John David and Brian came out to see as Jess got off the go-kart. Brian went around to the engine.

"First let's see if it'll start. Then we'll see if it has fire," Brian said.

They tried starting it with no results. Brian pulled the plug wire off and tried the trick I had showed them. Pulling on the cord yielded no spark. After many tries, there was finally a spark. He put the wire back on the spark plug and pulled the cord once more. This time the engine started.

"It's definitely an ignition problem," Brian said. "But why does it only happen sometimes?"

"I didn't notice it until I hit those bumps," Jess said.

"Yeah, come to think of it, it never happens until it gets bumpy," John David added.

"Maybe the points are just loose. Sometimes they make contact correctly, and sometimes they don't!," Brian predicted.

"There's only one way to find out," Jess said. "Let's go to work."

They pushed the kart back to the garage, and found some of John David's dad's tools. Soon they had the flywheel cover and the recoil-starting nut off. They found a steering wheel puller in the toolbox, and they used it to remove the flywheel.

Brian moved in to inspect the points. He pushed on one side with a stiffened finger. It gave under the pressure. It would only move slightly and would generally stick in the correct position.

"Looks like we've found it!" Brian said.

John David's dad also had feeler gauges that they used to set the proper gap between the points. Brian tightened the points securely. With a little more work, they had his engine back together again. One pull on the cord, and the engine fired right up.

After riding for a while, the boys began talking about the trail.

"Have you gotten your trail licenses yet?" John David asked.

"I didn't know you could get them yet," Jess answered.

"Yeah, they got the forms and the safety handbooks in Monday at the Chamber of Commerce. You just fill them out, show proof of a summer job or business, and get a parent's signature," he said. "Oh yeah, and a description of what you will be driving on the trail."

"What happens if you switch go-karts between now and the end of summer?" Jess asked.

"I guess you get a new license," he said.

"Or don't tell them," Jess said with a grin.

Jess and Brian left John David's and headed for home. On the way they decided to stop by Harvey's junkyard and look around for stuff to build their go-karts. Jess had a pretty good idea of how he wanted to build his. He just needed to find a really good motor to complete his design. He wanted one that would have a lot of power and go fast. He figured if the Orange Krate was fast with an 8-HP, then a 10-HP would be even better. So that's what he was on the lookout for.

Brian really hadn't given his that much thought. He knew he wanted his own, but he would be content to drive the Orange Krate for a while until he made up his mind. Whatever he got though, he knew he wanted to focus most of his attention on the motor.

When they got to the junkyard, Harvey and Sloppy were sitting under the awning of his shed as usual, watching the world go by. Harvey used to be a blacksmith. When he retired I got all his old business, but he kept his old equipment. To pass the time, he started doing lawnmower repair at his house. He ended up getting so much business he had to retire from that. He never sold out; he just sort of stopped doing it.

His lot was full of leftovers from his blacksmith shop, as well as the lawnmower business. There was years' worth of junk in that yard. Not only was there tons of junk leftover from his businesses, but Harvey just collected junk. It wasn't just worthless trash though; he had an intention for every piece in there. But, by this time in his life, he realized he would never get to all the projects he had planned out. Every now and then, he would sell off a few pieces of junk. Not to just anyone though. It had to be someone he really liked, to be sure the junk was going to a good home.

For some reason Harvey liked me--he had ever since the first time I met him. As my boys came up, they got to be around Harvey, as I would call on him to bail me out of a machining jam or two. He really liked Jess and Brian a lot. And that meant a great deal, because he didn't care for kids hanging around much.

The boys walked up under the awning of his old lawnmower repair shed and patted Sloppy on the head. They took a seat in some rusty old lawn chairs and greeted Harvey.

"How you boys doin'?," the old German asked.

"Pretty good," Jess responded. "We just come to see if we could look around, and maybe find some stuff to build go-karts out of."

"Da go-kart kids!," He laughed. "How's dat one you been working on comin'?"

"We finished it up Sunday, all except for the seat cushions. They're at the upholstery shop now," Brian told him.

"Dat stop you from ridin' it?," Harvey asked.

"Heck no!" Jess said. "We've almost worn it out again already."

They all laughed. Jess explained the conditions I had made for them to build their own after fixing up mine. He told Harvey that he would like to get one built by the time the trail opened. Jess explained that they had a little money saved up, and would need to get as much of their go-kart supplies out of the junkpile as possible.

Harvey wasn't very thrilled about the trail, but he was glad that the hardship rule was going to help the boys out. He told the boys they were welcome to look around the yard, and that he would give them a good deal on whatever they found.

Jess and Brian were excited when they walked through the gate. The piles of junk now seemed more thrilling to them than any amusement park could ever hope to be. They found all kinds of treasures. There were too many concepts to use on one go-kart. There was enough stuff there to build a whole fleet of go-karts.

There were even a few go-karts there already. Mostly just bare frames with no motors. Some were in decent shape, and others were bent and broken. They made several rounds through the yard, making note of everything they saw. Just when they thought they had found everything, they would notice another go-kart frame or tiller motor. Finally, Jess spotted what he had been looking for.

There was some sort of hydraulic equipment, with a big tank, and lots of piping on it. Nestled in the middle was a yellow air-cooled engine. He peered through the plumbing and read "Kohler" on the side. He looked closer and found "12 hp" on another place. He had found the motor he was looking for. He went back to ask Harvey about it.

Harvey drove them back to the treasure on his golf cart. Jess pointed it out as they drove up.

"That one with the hydraulic pump," Jess told him.

"Oh, yah. Dat was a job I did for old man Spates," Harvey said. "He had dat ol' pump unit for a long time till da engine didn't schnobble no more. He really needed a bigger engine for dat ting, but it wouldn't fit in da space. So I made his old engine more powerful." Harvey told them.

"It says it's a 12-horse on the side." Jess said.

"Ya, it was. But it's a lot more now. We tested it on a dynometer at nearly twenty before we put it on," Harvey said.

"Man!," Jess exclaimed.

"Ya, I bored out da cylinder and put a bigger piston in dar'. It had a domed top on it, so I had to make a special head, and heat treat it in my furnace. Da valves were made bigger. I put in a rod out of a motorcycle engine. I don't know where da crankshaft come from. It was layin' rusty in a load of junk I bought. I cleaned it up and made it work. After all dat, I had to build a special carburetors to make the dang ting run," Harvey told them.

"Is that why it has two air cleaners?," Brian asked.

"Ya, ya, for da two carbs! A primary and a secondary for when she needs more umph!," Harvey finished.

"How much do you want for her?," Jess asked, convinced that he had found his motor.

"I don't know if she gonna still work. For you, I'll take five bucks," Harvey said.

The boys made a few other selections of things they needed and got a total from Harvey. One treasure Jess was glad to find was a car stereo with tape deck and independently mounting speakers. They paid Harvey and took what they could carry, promising to come back later for the engine. Harvey assured them they had their work cut out for them in getting it out of the hydraulic unit.

Chapter 7

That Friday, the boys showed up at Harvey's with tools in hand. They dove in and went to tearing down all the hydraulic lines in their way. They had brought with them a wagon from the shop to bring the motor home. It was half full of things they were carrying home from the shop as well.

It was nearly dark before they got the engine loaded up and headed down the trail to the house. They had thought about going to Fred's, because there would be a lot of kids there on a Friday night. But even the best thick-crust, double pepperoni pizza wasn't gonna stop Jess from building the coolest go-kart in the world. Jess pulled the wagon down the trail in the fading sunlight while Brian pushed from behind.

At the shed, they unloaded the wagon and placed the big motor up on the bench. Jess checked the oil, and it still looked to be holding good. The spark plug wire was chewed in two by rats, so he knew it wouldn't start. Besides, engine was electric start, so he had no way of trying it anyway. But he tried turning it by hand. It didn't act like it was froze up any. It was just getting good compression.

After a thorough inspection, the boys believed that the engine was in reasonably good shape. It needed a new ignition coil and spark plug wire and a way to start it. They would see about all that in the morning. They were pretty beat from all the work it took to get the motor home.

They found their way to the auto parts store the next day where Carl sold them a new spark plug, coil and plug wire, and a motorcycle battery. They got back and installed the new parts. They found some good cable to replace the old battery cables. There was an old ignition switch under the bench, and they wired that in as well. With a little bit of gas, and a push of the button, the Frankenstein Kohler was "Alive."

"That makes three engines you've revived in one week!" Jess said to Brian.

He grinned at the compliment.

The Kohler had a deep throaty sound to it. It didn't sound

like most small engines. It sounded powerful. At a low idle, it almost sounded like it was going to die. But, when he pushed on the throttle linkage, it roared right up. Harvey had worked some serious magic on this motor.

At lunchtime, I brought home for them a few tools from the shop in town. I had an old tubing bender and tubing notcher I had only used for one job, plus a few odds and ends I also thought they might need while building their karts.

They put the engine on a worktable, and started laying out pieces of what was to be the frame of Jess's, kart. He was making measurements and sketches all day, trying to decide the best place to start. It was a little different building a go-kart from scratch. He made several attempts to start building the frame, but wasn't happy with any of them, and ended up ruining some of his materials.

When I came home in the afternoon, I could sense his frustration. After we ate, I went out to the shed with them to get them pointed in the right direction. I showed them how to properly use the tubing bender and notcher. I gave them a few pointers on how to clamp and weld pieces securely. And then I got out a spiral notebook. We ended up having a little go-kart class.

I knew we were going to be busy at the shop for a while with the start of summer coming, and I decided this was my last chance to really help them on their go-kart projects. I tried to show them everything I thought they would need, in a manner they could understand. I made notes in the notebook, along with several sketches. The book was full of mathematical calculations and formulas in which they could just plug in numbers and get the results needed. Fortunately both boys were good in math, so they were able to follow along. I even added a little information on geometry and trigonometry to help with the frame building.

With newfound wisdom, the boys proceeded slowly into the project. They were careful to make sure everything was done right the first time. They wanted this go-kart to be professional all the way.

Jess consulted the notebook frequently during the building

of his kart. He had to hunt me down a few times to clarify some of the notes I made. He added a few notes of his own to help him understand. It was coming along nicely. Brian helped a great deal, even though it wasn't to be his kart.

They had made a temporary jig to hold the wheels in place and achieve the right wheelbase that Jess wanted. They made a lot of measurements off of the Orange Krate for the sitting area. From there, they made changes to make it more suitable to Jess. One change was the steering support bars. Jess wanted them to be placed and sized to accommodate a tape playing car stereo he found in the junkyard.

It was taking longer than it did to rebuild the Orange Krate, but the boys didn't lose interest. The frame was now freestanding with steering. They took it down from the worktable and pushed it around on the ground. For a bare metal frame covered in weld beads, it was very cool looking. It would almost be a shame to paint over the evidence of such good construction.

The wheels really set off the frame. He had taken ordinary split-rim go-kart wheels and made some modifications. He used one side of the split rim for the inside half of the rim. And custom made the outside half. He did this by welding a flange on a short piece of aluminum pipe. He welded some fins around the center of the rim, and machined off all of the weld beads. Then he polished out all of the machining marks to make it look like they were made out of a solid piece of aluminum. They really shined from the polishing.

The back wheels were bigger than the front wheels, to give it a hot-rod look, and the back wheels were also slightly wider than the front. The seat sat very low to the ground. It had a low-profile racing look.

He was planning on mounting the engine in the middle of the rear, right behind the seat. This was so he could utilize the dual air cleaners to add another racing look. He was also planning on making a body for the frame--a sheet metal body made to look like the late model stock cars, with a steep slope in the front until it came up over his feet. From there it would slope gradually up to the steering wheel. The sides were to slope outward from the front, to the back of the seat. A hinged motor cover would be on the back. It would be slightly wider than the seat area, to allow air to move down the body and enter through scoops made by the engine cover to cool the engine. Custom-built stainless steel air cleaners were going to stick up out of the engine cover on either side of his head when sitting in the seat.

Two roll bars were added, one just above his feet and one above the back of the seat. The front one would support the body, and the back would hold the width of the body. He wanted the protection of a roll bar, but didn't want it to take away from the low profile look.

They got the engine mounted and referred back to my notes on gear ratios. They didn't know about the performance of this motor like I did about the 8-horse, because it was custom-built. So they ended up using the same ratio as the Orange Krate. They used the same belt clutch and pedal configuration as well.

For brakes, they decided not to go with a band. To save money, they went with the kind they saw on an old junker down at Harvey's. They consisted of two paddles on a bar. One paddle went in front of each rear tire. The bar had a lever that the brake cable hooked to. When you stepped on the brake pedal, it pulled the paddles into the wheels and made them stop. It was simple, and they could build it out of junk with little expense. Those kinds of brakes had a reputation for wearing out tires. But these tires were racing slicks, so it wouldn't matter as much.

When the frame was complete with the motor and clutch mounted, it was time to give her a test run before building the body and painting it. The motorcycle battery was mounted low, behind the seat, and it was wired to the starter. The starter and kill switch were mounted to a polished aluminum dash panel under the steering wheel. Outside the shop, Jess took his seat on his new kart and pushed the starter. The loping of the powerful engine was music to his ears. He let out the clutch and headed down the backpath towards the trail.

The kart spun out dramatically as he sped off. It felt at first as if he had a racing machine. He was very pleased.

Halfway down the path he wasn't as happy. The top-end speed was not as he had hoped. It showed a lot of spunk taking off, but couldn't back it up on the straightaway. He wondered if he had made the right choice on the gear ratio.

Back at the shed, he reviewed his calculations. He made another try, this time assuming the engine had more torque and fewer revolutions per minute (RPMs). With a new ratio, he found new pulleys to satisfy the calculations. Reassembled, he gave his kart another try.

This time, it was sluggish to take off. Once it was going, though, it would move very fast. Faster, even, than he cared to go on the path. He returned to the shed once more.

"I don't get it!," Jess said. "One works great for take off but is too slow. The other is plenty fast, but takes off to slow. Do you think I need something in the middle?"

"Well, it makes sense--like on a ten-speed just like dad said," Brian said. "But I don't think you want to meet in the middle. You want the best of both worlds, without sacrificing take off, or top end. Right?"

"Yeah, I guess so," Jess said.

"So why not have both?" Brian said.

"Yeah, but how?" Jess asked. "Wait! I get it."

"Just put both pulley setups on at once," Brian said.

"I can redo the idler pulley where it slides back and forth, and can be used to engage either belt!," Jess said. "I can make a lever to the side, with some linkage, that will move the idler from side to side when I push in the clutch. It will be like a gearshift and a two-speed transmission!"

The boys were excited at the prospect of having a two-speed go-kart. They went directly to work removing the newly-built clutch and reconfiguring it for the transmission.

Jess made the gearshift to the right side of his seat. It was made out of small, heavy tubing. He welded a piece of bolt with no head, into the end of the tube. He found an old "T" handle gearshift knob of mine under the bench. It was a custom-grip Hurst aluminum shifter. He threaded it and a jam nut onto the bolt on the end of the tube, and tightened the jam nut when he had it in the proper position to suit his grip.

He adjusted the linkage so that first and second gears were in comfortable positions for the gearshift. He made the slide for the idler so that it would slide easily while unengaged, but would lock in position while engaged. What locked them in position were notches that the idler arm fit into. When the clutch was disengaged, the idler arm was free of the notches. When the arm slid to the right position, in line with the belt, it landed into a notch that kept it in line with the belt.

He made a few modifications to the notches to make shift transitions smoother. The first was to put a curve to one edge of the notch between first and second. This was so that the arm could begin sliding while it was still being disengaged. The other was to put a stop, so he knew when he was in second.

They put it all back together and gave it a try. Jess fired up the kart and got ready to try it out. He popped the clutch and took off as before. But this time he felt the engine redline, where the go-kart wasn't going any faster. He then jabbed in the clutch, yanked back on the gearshift, and released the clutch again. It actually spun the tires again in the gravel on the path. He began going even faster, up to the speed where it felt scary. He reached the old iron gate by the trail and spun around to head back to the shed. As he entered the clearing behind the shed, he let off the gas and put it back in first. The engine roared as he down shifted and slowed until he stopped.

"This is the coolest go-kart ever!" He shouted at Brian.

"You should have seen how you took off! It was even cooler when you shifted to second!" Brian returned his enthusiasm.

They put the new kart in the shed and went back to work. Jess wanted to have it finished by the time the trail opened. He would have his work cut out for him with the sheet-metal body.

They used the sheet-metal tools at the shop to build the body. It was slow going, because the metal was more cantankerous than he had expected. I helped them when I could.

During the construction of the new kart, I took them to the Chamber of Commerce one day after school to apply for their trail licenses. I showed proof that they would be working for me at the shop and described the Orange Krate. They received a rulebook on trail etiquette and safe riding practices.

The end of school was approaching. The last day was on Friday, May 30. The trail was scheduled to be open on the following Saturday.

On the last day, Jess knew there was no way he would finish his new kart on time for the trail opening. His friends, John David and Shawn, were planning on meeting up at Fred's on Saturday with their go-karts. Jess wanted to surprise them with his new go-kart. But it looked like he would have to take the Orange Krate.

Chapter 8

Saturday the 31st came not a moment too soon. Jess was up early and could hardly wait to hit the trail. He was going to take the Orange Krate to meet with his buddies. Brian didn't mind letting Jess take it on the first day. Brian didn't have any friends that had go-karts anyway. Fred's wouldn't open until 10:00, but Jess couldn't wait. He decided to drive into town to meet up with John David.

He pushed the Orange Krate out of the shed and gassed it up. He checked the oil and the air cleaner. To be safe, he grabbed a handful of tools and put them in a small case that he tied onto the back with a bungee cord. Convinced he had everything, he headed out to John David's.

He flew down the backpath with excitement. He turned the corner after the old iron gate partially in a sideways slide. Making his way onto the trail, he went to town.

Harvey was out under his awning, so Jess stopped in to show him the go-kart. He informed Harvey about the progress on his new kart and how well "old Frankenstein" was working. After that, he continued to John David's.

When he got there, John David was getting his stuff together as well.

"I was just getting ready to come out to your place!" John David exclaimed.

"Beat you to it!" he returned. "I can hardly wait until ten. Why don't we head out to Shawn's now?"

John David agreed and, shortly, the two boys were headed east, out of town in the golden morning sunlight.

It was a few miles out to Shawn's farm. The boys were enjoying the ride. Jess's go-kart was a lot faster than John David's, but they went the same speed. Sometimes Jess would slow down to let John David pass, only to pass him right back.

There were a lot of hikers and bikers on the trail but, so far, no other go-karts. They were careful around the pedestrians, just like the trail handbook had said. Fortunately, most of the trail was long and straight, so they could see hikers well in advance. The hikers still seemed to be perturbed by the annoyance of the go-karts. The boys didn't care. If those "Yuppies" didn't like it, they could stay off the trail--or at least the Sumner section.

When they got to Shawn's farm, he was still busy doing chores. They had a few livestock, but mostly did crop farming. Shawn had to take care of the animals in the mornings. In the spring and fall, he stayed pretty busy driving tractor, putting in and harvesting crops. During the summer, he had most of the afternoon off.

Jess and John David helped Shawn finish his chores so they could get going. When they were finished, Shawn got cleaned up and serviced his go-kart. Shawn had a really cool go-kart. It was made during the "Dukes of Hazzard" days, because it was painted to look like the "General Lee." It was orange with a Confederate flag on the floorboard and the numbers "01" on both sides of the seat braces. The wheels were even replicas of those on the "General Lee" used on the TV show. The funniest part was that Shawn had tied two pink fuzzy dice to hang under the steering wheel.

When everybody was ready, they went off to cruise the trail until Fred's opened up. They went east for a while until they started getting close to Sand Flat. Then they decided to turn around and head back towards Sumner. The stretch between Sand Flat and Sumner was loaded with trees. There was only a little clearing around Shawn's place where there was farmland. Between Shawn's and Sumner was mostly wilderness.

There was a natural lake off to the left heading towards town. The trail group had built a little rest area with picnic benches overlooking the lake. Further down, on a long straightaway, was a place where the track bed had been carved into a hill on one side, and had a steep drop-off on the other. At the bottom of the drop-off was a small creek running alongside.

Past the straightaway was a bridge over Sumner Creek, followed by a curve, and then the old iron gate in the fence at the start of the backpath up our land. They past Jess's place and went to Fred's.

Fred had done some work in preparation for the trail opening. He tore down the raggedy fence and concreted in the section behind the restaurant. He made a long covered area with outside tables under it. The area with the tables was raised up like a median under the cover. On either side of the tables was room to park bicycles or go-karts. There was parking along both of the outside fences, too. There was a lane that went between the outside and inside parking rows. It made a "U" around between the back of the restaurant and the covered parking, and on out to the trail. It looked suspiciously like a miniature drive-in.

When Jess and the guys got there, they pulled into one side of the parking and looped around to the restaurant. They knew they were still early and could see that it was not open yet. So they looped back out and kept heading west on the trail.

They kept on through town and crossed the bridge over Highway 14. They went past the shop and gave a wave to some of the guys outside taking a break. They kept on going past town to see what they could see.

This whole time they were taking turns leapfrogging around. Jess still had the fastest go-kart, even with Shawn added to the group. They were having fun until they got a little further out of town.

They went passed a kid's house they knew, and he was outside. Zack Richter was his name, and none of the boys really liked him. He was the type of kid that no matter what you were doing or what you had, he could do it better or had something twice as good. He was always self-appointed captain of any sporting events that went on at school. He was always the first to call a foul on someone or yell at someone for screwing up.

Jess liked him the least. He didn't really like playing sports anyway but, every time he tried, Zack would make him so mad he would quit. It wasn't just sports though, he was like that about everything. Jess wasn't much on confrontation, so he would just avoid Zack, to keep from getting mad.

Zack was out by the trail when they went past. He waved down John David, because they played sports together a lot. John David stopped, so Shawn and Jess did, too.

Zack and John David talked about the trail being open and go-karting. Jess didn't add any to the conversation. John David knew Jess didn't like Zack, so he tried to get away by saying they had to get to Fred's.

"You guys are going to Fred's, huh?," Zack said. "I'll have to come down there after my dad comes back from town."

"What do you mean?" John David asked.

"My dad went to pick up my new go-kart from Sumner Small Engine," he said. "I was supposed to go with him but I didn't get up early enough."

"That's cool," John David said.

"I guess I'll see you guys down there!," Zack said as Jess started off in disgust.

It had put a damper on Jess's whole morning. He didn't want Zack running around with him. He was still upset when they got to Fred's.

They ordered a pizza and some Sun-drop and took their favorite booth by the window. So far they were the only ones there with go-karts.

"What's the matter with you?," John David asked.

"It's that Zack. Why did you have to stop and talk to him?," Jess asked disgustedly.

"I'm sorry. I know you don't like him, but we play football together. I couldn't just drive past," John David explained.

"I would have!" Shawn said.

"Oh, it's not your fault. He probably would've showed up anyway," Jess said. "It's just...I know he'll be up here bragging about his *new* go-kart. And he'll be acting like he knows everything about go-karts. I hate it when he gets like that."

"I know. But he doesn't, and you do. You can make him look like a doof," John David said, trying to cheer Jess up.

"Shut up!" Jess laughed, pushing John David on the shoulder. "No, I don't. I just know a little."

"Well, that's a lot more than Zack!," Shawn added.

They ate their pizza and enjoyed their time at Fred's until finally Zack showed up. He was driving exactly what Jess knew he would be, the Indy car look-alike from the small engine store. It looked pretty cool, but Jess knew it only had a 5-horse on it. He also knew the gear ratio wasn't set up to go very fast. Nevertheless, Zack came in bragging.

"Ain't that the best looking go-kart you've ever seen!" He said, boasting. "It's real fast, and it's brand new. Not like those old grass-burners you guys got!"

Jess turned away and acted like he had found something more interesting. Out of curiosity, the others couldn't resist going to look at the new kart. Jess followed reluctantly.

"This, my friends, is a high-performance go-kart. Don't get too close to it, you'll drool on it," Zack said, continuing his boasting. "It's not like those old junkers you have. It has a low-profile racing package, complete with street tires, polished spoiler, and a 5-horsepower race engine!"

"That's not a 'race engine,' it's just a plain old 5-horse," Jess said.

"Oh, yeah? Well, what've you got?" Zack said.

"The Orange Krate has an 8-horse," Jess told him.

"Orange Krate! What does it run on? Orange juice?" Zack laughed at Jess's kart.

"No, but I bet it would run better on juice than yours runs on gas!" Jess said in frustration.

"I don't think so. Mine is brand new. And that old thing will probably fall apart if you go over 5 miles an hour! I don't care if you did give it a new coat of paint to try to hold it together," Zack added, perturbed that anyone might think Jess was right.

The boys were gonna leave to drive around some more. Zack told them to stay while he got a slice of pizza, and he would go with them. Reluctantly, the boys waited. Finally they were on their way again. Zack made sure to push his way in front first. He turned right out of Fred's and headed east in the direction of Jess's.

As they went, Shawn and John David started up their game of leapfrog again, where each one passed the others and took a turn in the lead. Every time John David or Shawn tried to pass Zack, he got all competitive and sped up. He acted like it was a race instead of fun. Jess saw what was going on and couldn't resist. He tromped on the gas and began to pass. When he got to Zack, Zack wasn't going to let him pass. But he had no choice. Jess was around him and in the lead before he could react.

Out of the corner of his eye Jess could see Zack's stiffened leg riding the gas as hard as he could. Jess could also see furrowed brow and look of bewilderment on Zack's face as if trying to figure out just how this old, kid maintained go-kart could be passing his brand new one that was running at full speed.

The answer was of course that he was not in fact running at full speed but rather the full factory setting. As Brian had anticipated, most kids with go-karts would not know they could run beyond the factory range of speed. He knew his invention would clearly give Jess an advantage if any challenge came up. The toggle switch action just added the perfect effect of mystery.

Jess never let on that anything was out of the ordinary for him or his kart. He just looked straight ahead, expressionless as he overtook Zack. Inside he felt like he might erupt in triumph. As he pulled back into the lane in front of Zack he could no longer suppress the broad grin that was spreading across his face. He had beaten Zack at something. In fact, he had flat whooped Zack at something. This wasn't something you could just buy from the store. This wasn't something popularity could give you an advantage at. This was a solid victory for the McCormick brothers. Jess felt a welling sense of pride for his little brother and the job they had done together on the kart. He knew this was going to be a great summer.

In the thrill of the moment, Jess no longer feared the wild acceleration of the engine but welcomed it. He kept speeding far ahead of the group and didn't let off until he was out of sight around a long curve.

Beyond the curve Jess spotted a trailside park that the

Dennis R. Van Vleet

yuppies had built. He decided to flip off the boost switch and pull in to park. He had made a big statement back on the trail and he was ready to see Zack's full reaction.

When they got out to the lake, Jess stopped in the trailside park. The others followed in behind. Jess got off of his kart grinning. Zack immediately began protesting Jess' passing him.

"I wasn't ready when you did that!," Zack shouted.

"Ready for what? We were just playing leapfrog," Jess told him. "It wasn't a race."

The other boys dismissed the incident. Everyone but Zack was talking and having a good time. Jess felt good again because this was one thing Zack couldn't take control of. Zack was still grumpy. He kept bringing up what happened.

"Why do you keep bringing it up?" Shawn finally confronted him. "So Jess is faster than you. Big deal. He's faster than all of us. Get over it."

"Nuh uh. He ain't faster than me! He cheated!" Zack yelled.

"Cheated at what?" Jess asked in a raised voice. "It wasn't a race!"

"Well…" Zack started.

"Well, nothing. It wasn't a race. But if you want to race, I'll race you. Then maybe you'll shut up!," Jess told him.

"A race? Yeah, I'll race you. There's no way that old thing can beat me!" Zack said.

"We'll see," Jess told him confidently. "We'll go down a little ways towards town on this straightaway. We can start at the abandoned gravel
pit road. It's about 1/8 mile from there to the Sumner Creek Bridge. The first one to make it from the gravel pit road to the bridge wins. Got it?"

"Oh, you're on! But that old…" Zack started.

"Save it for the race!," Shawn said cutting him off.

All of them drove back to the gravel pit road. They lined up even with the road. You could see there was no one coming down the straightaway. Shawn got off his kart to flag them.

58

Standing out in front of and between the two go-karts, side by side on the trail, Shawn held up his hand.

"Ready...Set...Go!" Shawn shouted, as he lowered his hand.

Jess had his engine revved way up as he held in the clutch. The engine had a lot of momentum when he popped the clutch. He had a fast takeoff from the start. Zack couldn't do that with his centrifugal clutch, so he had a sluggish start. Jess had him from the get go. Zack didn't have a chance of winning, even though he tried clear to the end. Jess kept going past the bridge and headed back to Fred's.

John David and Shawn, and of course, Zack followed, too. When they got there, Zack wanted to protest again. Several of their classmates were hanging out in the restaurant by this time.

"Look, you lost! Accept it. You probably want a rematch. But you won't get one," Jess told him. "We can run that stretch all day long, and you'll never beat me. Not with a 'stock' go-kart."

Flustered and embarrassed, Zack left and sped off towards home. Jess felt good, he thought he wouldn't have to worry about Zack for the rest of the summer. He even told John David so.

"I wouldn't bet on it. I know Zack, and his dad, too. His dad is just as competitive. Zack will go home and cry about it, and his dad will buy him the biggest engine at Sumner Small Engine."

Jess knew the biggest engine that Sumner sold was a stock 10 HP.

"Bring it on. I'll be ready," Jess said, knowing he would have his new kart finished before then.

Brian walked in about then and got something to eat. Jess let him drive the go-kart to the shop. He decided to walk to work.

Chapter 9

When both Jess and Brian finally got home, they went straight to work on the new go-kart. The business of sharing one wasn't going to work for very long.

The sheet-metal body was roughly finished, it just needed to be riveted to the frame. Jess wanted to make an access door in the front, to get to a storage area in the front floorboard. They also had to work on the hinged motor cover in the rear. It would need to hinge far enough out of the way to service the engine. They had to make some way of latching it closed so the wind wouldn't flip it open. After that, the body would require a little trimming to make it look right.

The first step was to strip and sandblast the frame and then paint it. Jess wanted to go with an red-orange color for the frame and roll bars, and moonlight blue for the body. The engine would be high heat Hemi Orange.

Jess took his time painting the frame and body. He even started out by putting a coat of primer on the metal. He put several coats of paint on and gave each coat ample time to cure. He knew he didn't have a lot of time, but he wanted it to be perfect.

He also took his time reassembling the kart, making sure not to scratch the fresh paint job. Before he put the body on, he took some time to mount his car stereo down between the steering supports, between his legs. He wired power to it and ran an excess length of speaker wires under the seat and tied them up loosely to the roll bars.

When the body was riveted on, he made some additions to the seat area. To his left, he mounted a little box he had found that would work for holding small junk like tapes or small tools. He also added the drink holder, just the right size to hold a longneck bottle of Sun-drop. The last thing was to mount the speakers.

The stereo speakers he had mounted with a little swivel bracket. He clamped the brackets to the roll bars on either side of his head, and mounted and wired the speakers. They weren't very big speakers so it wouldn't hurt his ears, but it was just enough that he could hear them over the sound of the engine. Plus, he could turn them up when the go-kart was off and hear them from a distance.

When it was all finished, he had to take it for a test run. Satisfied with its performance, he put the new kart back in the shed. He and Brian spent the rest of the evening just admiring it.

By this time it was Wednesday. Jess drove the Orange Krate down to Fred's to see what was going on. His buddies were there hanging out. He sat down to get the word.

The story of the race between Jess and Zack had spread all over town. The part witnessed by the kids at Fred's stuck out the most. Everyone knew how Zack was and knew there would be a rematch. Rumors were stirring about the new go-kart Zack was getting. John David had heard, from a good source, that Zack was seen with his dad buying the 10-horse from Sumner Small Engine.

He had also heard that it would be ready on Thursday. The big rematch was to go down at noon. Jess hadn't told anyone about his new kart. He wanted to really make an appearance.

That night, Jess took the kart out practicing. He wanted to make sure he had the shifting down, so that he never lost any power. There was a full moon out, so he could see down the trail. There was no one out at that time of night, and there was no danger of anyone seeing the big surprise he had planned.

He went out to the spot where they had raced before. He figured the race would go from the bridge to the gravel pit road this time, since they would probably be coming from Fred's. So that is the stretch he practiced. Brian came with him and brought a stopwatch. He stood at the end of the stretch and flagged Jess with a flashlight. He started the timer right when he flashed the light and stopped when Jess got to the road.

Jess floored his new kart at the flash of the light and screamed off the line. It was an impressive sound as he shifted to second, but it was even more impressive when the secondary carburetor kicked in. Closer and closer he came to Brian. At the gravel pit road, Jess was coming toward Brian so fast, and with a noise so loud that Brian actually stepped back out of fear. When the kart flew past, its sound dropped off and Brian was left standing there with his hair blown back and his clothes ruffled in the wind.

Jess kept practicing until his time leveled off and stayed constant. He figured he and the kart were ready. They went back to the shed and put her up for the night.

Brian left first the next day and took the Orange Krate to scout out Fred's. He found the guys and sat down with them at the booth. "What's the deal. Why are you driving the Orange Krate?" John David asked. "Don't Jess know he's supposed to race today?"

"Well, yeah. But he sent me down to find out if Zack is gonna show up," Brian told them.

"He'll show up. His little toadies have been spreading rumors all morning for him," Shawn said. "He has a new motor for sure, a 10-horse Briggs. I sure hope the Orange Krate will beat it. I don't want to put up with him braggin' all summer. It's been peaceful these past few days."

"I don't know. He's probably changed his gear ratio, too. I don't think the 8-horse will beat Zack," Brian told them.

"Oh, no! Don't tell me that!" Shawn said.

"I better call Jess and tell him what's up." Brian went to the pay phone.

Fifteen minutes later they were still talking. The restaurant was filling up by this time. A lot of people heard about the race and all the go-kart news, and came down to check out the action. Brian kept watching the trail for Jess or Zack, hoping Jess would get there first.

"Is he walking down here or what?" Shawn said impatiently to Brian. "I sure hope he makes it. I'd hate for you to have to race Zack."

"Hey!" Brian said in his defense. "I can drive just as good as Jess! Besides, here he is now."

Jess rounded the corner and turned into Fred's in his new go-kart. He was downshifting, so the engine made a loud noise that everyone inside noticed. He came around the "U" and quickly stopped in front of the door. He revved her up one time, locked the brake and got out. John David and Shawn immediately got up and came outside. Almost everyone inside followed.

"Where in the world did you get that?" John David asked excitedly.

"It's just a little project I've been working on," Jess said proudly.

"What size motor is that?" Shawn asked. "It's huge!"

Jess reached in and hit the kill switch. Then he unfastened the rear cover and hinged it open, revealing his power plant.

"This is a modified 12 horsepower Kohler. The only thing "stock" left on it is the block. The rest is all customized to get maximum performance," Jess told them.

Everyone was gathering around to check it out. Jess even had to back up to get out from the mob. He was standing in front of the crowd, close to the Orange Krate. Just then, his old buddy showed up. Zack came riding into Fred's followed by a couple of his toadies on their new go-karts.

He roared up, stopping only inches from Jess.

"I hear you've been bragging all over town that you think you can beat me in a race!" Zack said.

"Not that I think I can, that I did. And I can!," Jess countered.

"Well, maybe you did. But that puny 5-horse was a lemon. You're ancient Orange Krate won't beat me now. And I aim to prove it!"

Jess looked back at Brian.

"What do you think? Think the Orange Krate'll take him?" Jess asked him.

Brian shook his head.

"My engine man says you got him with that 10-horse. I guess the Orange Krate ain't the fastest kart in town anymore." Jess told Zack.

"You're not even gonna race me?," Zack said, as if to call Jess a chicken.

"Oh, I'm gonna race you, but I'm gonna use *my* go-kart,"

Jess told him.

Jess stepped aside, and so did the crowd, to reveal the new, sheet-metal-bodied go-kart. Zack hadn't even seen it, because he was so focused
on the crowd's reaction to his challenge, instead of what they were around.

Zack's jaw fell open.

"You bought a new kart?" He said in disbelief.

"No, I built it," Jess said coolly. "I think you know where to go."

Jess closed the engine cover, only allowing Zack to have a short peek at the engine. He latched one side, while Brian did the other. Jess climbed in and fired it up.

"See ya at the bridge!" Jess hollered back as he popped the clutch and squealed off out of Fred's parking lot. It sounded awesome when he shifted to second hitting the trail.

The crowd was looking at Zack to see what he was going to do. He looked back at his friends as if to ask if they knew. They just shrugged their shoulders, because they didn't.

Zack had no choice. He hit the gas and headed to the race spot. The whole crow followed behind. The go-karts first, followed by bicycles. The rest tried to run, hoping they might at least see the tail end of the race.

When Zack got there, Jess was right in line with a white mark he and Brian had painted on the trail about fifty feet past the bridge. They measured out exactly 1/8 mile from that line to another line even with the gravel pit road.

The other five go-karts went around and parked off to the side. Shawn came out to flag again. Jess was revving his engine.

He looked over at Zack who was looking straight ahead.

Zack had spent the week convincing everybody that he was gonna cream Jess. He was starting to think that you just can't buy your way to the top.

Jess gripped the wheel tightly with one hand and the shifter with the other. He squeezed it tight and rolled his hand. He hadn't been this nervous the last time they raced because there hadn't been this much hype leading up to it. He had all the faith in the world that Harvey's Kohler would do it; he just wanted so badly to win.

Shawn raised his arm and began the countdown.

Jess revved the engine and flexed his clutch leg, getting ready to release. He gripped the shifter as tight as he could.

Shawn gave the countdown.

"Ready...Set...Go!"

Jess let out the clutch and tromped the gas. He had a good take-off from the line. The engine was almost up to redline.

Zack had a sluggish start, but he was coming out of it pretty quickly. He was gaining on Jess, and his front tires were almost even with Jess's seat.

Just about the time Zack was starting to think he might actually pass Jess, the Kohler redlined.

Jess stabbed the clutch pedal and pulled back so hard on the shifter it felt like he bent the lever. When it hit the stop, he let out the clutch and the engine took hold again.

For an instant, Jess' go-kart slowed from the transition from first to second gear. Zack had made it dead even with Jess. But as the engine took hold, Jess began to fly past Zack. He had several kart lengths on Zack by the time they reached the other line.

Jess had clearly won the race. It was evident even to the few stragglers showing up on bikes. Jess and Zack made their turn around in separate spots and headed back to Fred's.

Everyone cheered as Jess came past. They were real quiet when Zack came past, but snickered and laughed after he was by. The crowd followed Jess back to the pizza place except Zack. He just went slowly to the house. He acted as if his buddies should come with him, but even they were taken in by the excitement of the day and wanted to hang out with everyone else and talk about go-karts.

Zack was pretty quiet after that. He didn't hang out or anything. No one saw much of him, not even his toadies. The story was that his dad got so mad about spending all that money and Zack not winning, that he grounded him for the rest of the summer. But you know how rumors go.

Everyone back at Fred's was interested in how Jess was

able to build his own go-kart like that. He told of how he and Brian were allowed to use the power tools at the shop. He gave credit to Brian for doing most of the work on the engines, but took plenty of credit for being the frame and drivetrain expert.

Some kids thought maybe the boys could build a go-kart for them. Others wanted to know if they could fix up their old junkers. John David and Shawn wanted to know if they could just make theirs go faster.

The excitement of the race and the mounting number of go-karts on the trail made everyone want one. Jess's and Brian's inexpensive junkyard revival skills made owning one seem that much more attainable to the kids now. Go-kart fever had officially hit Sumner. And soon to follow was the entire Hardship stretch of the Prichard-Bay Trail.

Chapter 10

All summer I let the boys have the mornings off, just like the weekends during the school year. The next morning after the big race, they were out in the shed early. John David had come by so Jess and Brian could take a look at his kart.

He wanted to ditch the 3.5-horse and get a bigger motor. They looked it over as John David thought of more modifications he wanted to make.

"What kind of motor did you have in mind?" Brian asked.

"I want one of those!" John David said, pointing to Jess's kart.

"I don't think you'll find another one of those. It's a one-of-a-kind."

"Well, how about a regular 10- or 12-horse?" John David asked.

"I don't know. They aren't really that easy to come by, and they are kind of expensive to get parts for. For the money, you'd probably do best starting out with a 5- or an 8-horse Briggs," Brian told him. "They are easy to get parts for, and Harvey had a ton of them down there. Besides, I've been thinking about all this size bit. I mean, Jess's go-kart is *really* fast, but that may be just because of the modifications and the transmission. I wonder if you can't get enough speed with a smaller, faster-turning motor and the right gears."

"Well, you're the motor master. Why don't you find out?," Jess asked him. "We can get an old five-horse and rebuild it. You can modify it to turn faster, and I'll make the modifications to the drivetrain. If we can make it work, maybe our buddy here will cough up some of that lawn mowin' money he's been savin' for a rainy day!"

"Will you take my old motor in trade for part of it?" John David asked.

"I suppose we could. I'm sure we can find someone who would be happy just to have a working motor for a ratty frame we put together. And when they get bored with that one, we'll take it back in trade again, and give *them* an upgrade."

"Sounds like a good plan to me!" Brian told him.

"Sounds like you're gonna be taking a lot of allowance money this summer to me!" John David added.

With that, all three go-karts headed down the backpath to Harvey's.

It didn't take long to find a 5-horse once they got inside the yard. There was practically a pile of them. Brian picked out what he thought was the best one. They paid Harvey for it and told him their plan to get more speed from a smaller motor. Brian was hinting for pointers on how to do it.

Harvey was more than glad to help. He was a little funny about it though. He gave all three boys some general information, but he waited to catch Brian by himself to let him know some real secrets. Brian felt privileged to be getting trade secrets from a small-engine master.

Jess explained their hopes of getting a lot of go-kart business over the summer. Harvey went in his shed and got a few extras he wanted to give the boys. It was boxes of old small-engine repair and parts manuals that had lots of repair and trouble shooting tips in them.

They loaded up what they could and pulled a wagon back for the rest. Using one of the manuals Harvey gave them, they found the rebuild kit part number for the new engine they had just bought. Jess made a trip to the auto parts store to see if Carl had one.

The auto parts store wasn't on the trail, but there was an alleyway like the one behind John David's house, that led from the trail to the store. Jess just had to be very careful crossing the residential streets along the way. The townspeople were OK with go-karts on the trail, but they might not be OK with them in town.

Jess made his way up and parked in the back. He went in and greeted Carl, asking for the rebuild kit by part number. Carl was able to walk straight to it. He started to hand it to Jess, but then pulled it back.

"What are you doing with all these parts?" Carl asked suspiciously.

Jess proceeded to tell Carl about the go-kart building, the

race, and the possibly lucrative business he and Brian were getting into.

"So you might be buying a lot of parts this summer, huh?" Carl asked.

"We hope to," Jess said.

"You know, kids aren't usually known for having a lot of money," Carl told him

"I know, but most of our stuff will come from the junkyard, so it won't cost much. The only thing expensive is our time and, well, new parts," Jess said.

"I tell you what, since you are a new business, I'll cut you a break. I'll sell you new parts at my cost. I'll even start a ticket for you, where you only have to pay every two weeks. How's that sound?," Carl asked Jess.

"That would be great!" Jess exclaimed.

He put the parts on a ticket and went back to the shed.

Jess and Brian went to work on John David's go-kart. Brian started working miracles on the junkpile 5-horse. Jess removed the old 3.5-horse and began modifying the mounting brackets to fit the new power plant. John David hung around to watch and help when he could.

They had several visits by the end of the morning. It was kids wanting work done similar to John David. Some just wanted to hang and be around the go-kart action.

When they went to lunch at Fred's there were still more kids wanting to know about go-karts and go-kart modifications. It was kind of a rush for the boys to be the center of the whole go-kart scene. People would say, "Do you think if I got you some tubing and an old motor, you could put something together for me?"

They would say, "Sure. Bring what you got by the shop in the morning and we'll see what we can do." (They began referring to the shed as their shop now.)

They began promising out a lot of work. It wasn't long before they were covered over in work.

Just about every kid in town who could drive a go-kart was thinking of ways to get one. Most of them came down to needing money and parental permission. Also, to cruise the trail, they would need a job. Luckily, these things all worked hand in hand.

Getting a job seemed to be the key to getting a go-kart. With the job, came of course, money, along with an excuse to get a trail license. The job also meant proving responsibility to parents, to get their permission to have a go-kart. The only problem was not having enough kid jobs, for the number of kids that wanted go-karts.

The main available job to kids was mowing lawns. The first problem there, was that there were only so many lawns to mow in Sumner and the surrounding areas. The second problem was needing a lawn mower. Jess and Brian were able to help out some on this part. They would take junk lawn mowers and make them run just enough to get the kids by. All the kids hoped for was that the junkers would pay for themselves and earn enough money to get a go-kart. And maybe save up a little for gas.

But John David was becoming king of mowing. Most of the lawns being hired out to mow were being mowed by John David's business. He had expanded his territory to encompass Sumner, Shady Grove and Sand Flat. He had to take on several employees and add more mowers. Jess and Brian fix up a riding mower for him and added a special road gear capable of going as fast as a go-kart.

Other avenues of employment were cleanup jobs, picking sweet corn or berries, and hauling hay. There was a new up-cropping of snow cone and lemonade stands. One group of kids that played in the cadet band at school even started a rock group. It wasn't very profitable, but they borrowed some equipment and Fred agreed to pay them to play in the back room on Friday and Saturday nights. They also managed to rustle up some gigs in Sand Flat and Shady Grove.

Others had a different plan. They got their parents to cover for them on the job part. (The trail authority didn't do in depth research into how stable any of the kid jobs were.) And did as much junk hustling as they could. Their goal was to get enough junk together to build a go-kart, along with enough to trade to get it built.

There was so much go-kart work that they had to get up early and work clear up till lunchtime. A quick bite to eat, and they were on their way to my shop in town. After supper, they were back out in the shed working on go-karts again, sometimes until late into the night.

It was beginning to be a lot of work. Most kids would have rather spent their summer just lying around, rather than working their guts out. But the boys loved it. They were getting better at what they did, and were learning much more. The biggest challenge was not making other kids' go-karts faster than their own with what all they were learning. After all, they had a reputation to uphold.

As far as their own go-karts, Brian finally figured out what he was going to do about his own, and Jess found a name for his. They had taken in on trade an old, funny looking little frame. Someone practically gave it to them, because they didn't think it was worth much. The steering wheel was metal, and what tires it had were made out of hard rubber. It was so old there was no paint left on it--it was only rust.

There was only a hint of blue paint on the seat back and floorboard, where there were faded and worn decals. They were yellow with red and green graphics, and you could just barely make out the words, "Yazoo Dragster." Brian said there was something about the decal that made him want it.

He decided he liked the 5-horse Briggs and Stratton the best and had some ideas he wanted to try on one. So he bought a junkpile 5-horse and kept the Dragster for himself, working on it when he could. He wanted to do an all-out restoration on it, along with a few upgrades.

The story about the race between Jess and Zack was like a legend on the trail. Somehow the story spawned the name "Heatseeker" for Jess' new kart. It was said that's because it ran for the finish line like a heat-seeking missile.

Now, all of this extra work was making their performance at my shop suffer. They were never there on time, and their minds were hardly ever on their work. They spent most of their time making drawings and designs for go-kart frames and modifications. I began noticing this behavior, so I spoke to them about it.

"I thought getting you that go-kart might be a mistake. But I gave you the benefit of the doubt and did it anyway. Now look at what has happened," I said. "All you guys do is play with and daydream about go-karts."

"But, dad! You don't understand," Jess told me. "We aren't playing with go-karts. We've been working our guts out doing custom work for other people. We're snowed under with work right now. We can't build or fix them fast enough."

"You have?" I said puzzled. "I thought one wasn't enough, so you were spending all your time dreaming up new ones that you wanted."

"No, all this is for other people," Jess said.

"Are you charging enough for what work you do?"

"We are making more than we do here. We wouldn't do it for free, you know."

I started to realize how cool what they were doing was. They were doing the kind of stuff I always wanted to do when I was their age. I was so swooned by the idea of a custom go-kart shop run by kids that I made them an offer.

"So you are snowed under with your own work, and you make more than you do here. Then what are you doing working here?"

"Well, you need us here, and it is our responsibility to work at the family business," Jess told me.

"Sounds like you have a family business of your own. I'll tell you what--I can get some of the guys to do your work for now. Why don't you take the summer to work at your own shop. If we get busy, and I need you, I'll ask you to come back for a while. I'll even pay what you make at the go-kart shop," I offered.

"Cool!" Brian exclaimed.

They finished what they were doing and loaded up to go back to the go-kart shop.

Chapter 11

The first thing they decided to do, now that they were full-time go-kart mechanics, was to make some improvements around the shop. First of all, they needed a better way to haul parts back from the junkpiles. The old radio flyer wagon they had been using, wasn't holding up too good tied behind a go-kart.

Jess decided to build a two-wheeled trailer that was big enough to haul a whole go-kart if needed. It would be used mostly for engines and scrap steel and the occasional junk frame.

He made the axle out of a piece of shaft and used some wheels from the junkpile. The tongue and frame were made out of square tubing instead of round, so as to not use up valuable go-kart stock. The floor was made out of scrap wood from old pallets. He made up a hitch on the end of the tongue, and mating drawbars on both the Orange Krate and the Heatseeker. Although he didn't really like the idea of pulling a trailer with his racing kart, it did have the most power to pull.

The second improvement was to help gain a little extra money. There were plenty of kids hanging around the shop spending their hard-earned money having go-kart work done. The rest were just hanging around for free. Brian had a plan to fleece the loiterers. He had his eye on an old soda machine at my shop.

It was a Sun-drop machine that served the old long neck bottles. It was the kind that had a long, skinny glass door to the bottles. You made your selection by pulling on the bottle you wanted. The machine belonged to me, and I just got tired of dealing with the returnable bottles, so we switched to a can machine.

Brian made a deal with me to move it home to the go-kart shop. He also got in touch with Stanley from Teague's Beverage, the local area bottler and distributor of Sun-drop. They serviced several businesses in town, including my shop,

Fred's, and now the new go-kart shop.

Speaking of the go-kart shop, it needed a name. And that is another improvement they made. They found a name, Go-Kart Alley Kustom Kart Shop. It came from the nickname that the yuppie trail hikers had given to the Sumner section of the trail. They called it Go-Kart Alley, due to the rise in go-kart traffic on the trail.

They made a sign to put out by the old iron gate on the trail. That way they might get even more business, in case there were go-karts traveling through from Sand Flat and Shady Grove that didn't know about Sumner's resident go-kart wiz kids. They painted a big piece of sheet metal gloss black for the base of the sign, then had their friend, Roman, paint the lettering.

Roman was a good artist and had an airbrush kit. The boys let him use the air compressor to power his new, never-been-used kit. He was glad to finally get to use it. Roman did such a good job painting the sign that the boys struck a deal with him to do all of their custom paint jobs.

The sign was topped with a picture of a go-kart made to look like the Orange Krate. It was a back/side view of it pointing down a long trail lined with tall trees that vanished to a point in the distance. Underneath in big, bold, chrome letters it read "Go-Kart Alley." In smaller letters under that was "Kustom Kart Shop."

To compliment the new sign, they added some more to the pole they erected by the trail. Harvey had tons of old small-engine signs in his yard. He was more than happy to part with a few of them. It looked very professional to show all the different kinds of engines they serviced at their shop. There were even more up on the walls of the shop; including names like; Briggs and Stratton, Kohler, Tecumseh, and of course, Sun-drop.

They had made flyers to put up on all of the bulletin boards along the trail with their name, number, and location. They were able to receive calls now, because there was a phone jack in the shed on the same line as the house. The only problem was that their mom would always answer the phone if it was for them. And they would always answer if it was for her. So she decided that, if they answered and it was for her, they should just have the caller call back. She would do the same if it was for them. It was annoying, but it was the cheapest way to get a phone.

They were in business now, for sure. Their advertising was paying off, and soon their extra time at the go-kart shop was consumed with work the same as before.

They did, however, take more time to have lunch and hang out at Fred's at noon and in the evenings. After all, that is where they got most of their business. Fred's was the go-kart center of the whole trail. They always carried some tools with them, because there was always someone there in need of some repair.

Zack's buddies still hung around Fred's without their fearless leader. They didn't really get around Jess that much, but they learned enough secondhand that they were able to keep up with the go-kart crowd. Jess was pretty much king of the trail, and everybody respected that. Of course, Jess was just as nice and courteous as ever to everyone he was around.

Most of the people at Fred's knew Jess and Brian and their work. Most of the go-karts there were either built, fixed, or modified by Jess and Brian. But there were a growing number of go-karts on the trail from out of the area, and the Heatseeker was getting its share of challengers.

Almost every evening, Jess was making his way out to the stretch outside of town where they liked to race. Never was he beat. He, with the help of Brian, kept the Frankenstein Kohler running in top shape. Plus, he was so good at finessing his two-speed transmission that nobody could take him.

One day, he was challenged on a parts run to Sand Flat. Brian needed a carburetor kit that Carl was sold out of, so Jess went to get one from the parts store there. It was a small bunch of parts so he just took the Heatseeker with no trailer.

On the way back, he ran up on a congested area of the trail with several hikers and bikers. He was patient and putted slowly behind with no opportunity to pass. During this, a sleek black go-kart had come up behind Jess.

Dennis R. Van Vleet

This go-kart was not patient. He was swerving back and forth in the lane. He would gun the motor only to stop just short of hitting Jess. Jess was getting irritated with this jerk's behavior.

As soon as there was a chance to pass, the black go-kart gunned it to get around. Jess saw this and pushed the Heatseeker out to pass in front of him. Once he was around the hikers, Jess decided to drop back into his lane, slow it down a bit, and let the ignorant driver around to go on.

But the driver only dropped in front of Jess going intentionally too slow. Every time Jess would start to pass, he would speed up again. Jess was fairly certain he could take him, but didn't want to indulge in the silly game. If he wanted a race, he would have to get it in the proper manner.

As they approached a stop sign where the trail crossed a one-lane country road, the other driver pulled into the opposing lane. Jess pulled up next to him at the stop sign and looked over to get a look at this jerk. He was grinning smugly at Jess when he came to a stop.

"I guess it's true what they say!," The driver called over. "You've got the fastest kart in Sumner."

"We'll, I've never..." Jess started.

"I said in Sumner!" The driver interrupted.

It was clear he wanted a race. Jess didn't bother to argue with him. There was only one way to wipe the smart look off his face. He just took a glimpse to see there were no cars coming on the road, and looked straight ahead down the trail. He poised his body and readied the controls to race. There was no one there to flag them, so Jess just waited for the other driver to start.

Sure enough, the driver hit the gas and began to take off. Jess gave the Heatseeker all that it had. Shortly, he was going around his challenger and noticing a different expression on his face. Jess kept on going and didn't slow down. Well into second gear, he looked back to see the black go-kart turning around to head back to Sand Flat. Jess laughed to himself about how sure that guy was about beating him. It was obvious that he had no clue what it took to win races. And it wasn't ego.

Jess kept going at full throttle back to the shop. There was a hiker or two that he just went around as long as he could see well around them.

Halfway home he came up on a whole group of people riding bikes.

He could tell from a distance that they were from the city. They had all funny-colored bikes with matching riding outfits on, and wearing every piece of safety equipment known to man. It was as if they couldn't enjoy a simple ride through the country without spending a bunch of money and four hours getting ready to go. They were laden with food and water as if they were riding across the desert. It was almost comical to Jess how they were.

He really didn't care much for this kind of folk so, as an act of defiance to their ways, he decided to blow past them at full throttle.

Just as he was about to them, a girl on one of the back two bikes turned to see the source of the oncoming noise. When she did, everything he had thought about the bikers flew out the window. She was the cutest girl he had ever seen. She looked to be his age and had beautiful dark hair, with a small spot of freckles bridging her nose.

She smiled a bit at his bad boy image and cool kart. A combination of that smile, those freckles, the speeding, along with the perfect speeding music blaring from his tape player, gave him an adrenalin rush like he had never felt. At that moment, he felt like the coolest kid in the world.

Feeling kind of dumb after he did though, he didn't know how he would get to see her again. So he pushed on, not slowing down. Shortly, he came upon the lake, trailside-park. Shawn was parked there talking to another friend of theirs. Jess whipped in and slid up next to them on the gravel. He looked first to see that he was out of sight of the biking group. Opening the hood to expose his chrome-accessorized power plant, Jess entered the conversation as if he were really interested in talking. With his thumbs hanging in his pockets, trying to look cool leaning against a picnic table, he kept checking the trail to see when the girl would arrive.

When they finally started riding up, the adults looked down their noses at the boys and their go-karts. They obviously didn't approve of them being on the trail; especially Jess, for how he had passed them. Jess didn't care. He was too busy looking back at the end of the line of bikes.

She was talking to and giggling with the girl riding next to her, but she turned to see if Jess was there. She spotted him and quickly looked back to her friend, and they both giggled. When she looked again, Jess gave a little sweeping wave with his hand low. She waved back with her fingers.

Not long after she had passed, he shut his hood and said, "Later!" and was gone.

This time he eased up on them slowly, putted up alongside, and made small talk. He asked her name first.

"Josie," she replied. "This is my cousin Lisa."

Jess could've cared less about her cousin. "You guys aren't from around here, huh?"

"No, they are from Bay City. I am from Jamestown. I'm just along for the ride," Josie said.

"Where in the world is Jamestown?," Jess asked.

"It's just the other side of Sand Flat. I go to school in Sand Flat," Josie told him.

"Well, I'm from Sumner," Jess said.

"I know. You're Jess McCormick," she replied. "And that is Heatseeker. The fastest go-kart on the trail."

Jess got butterflies in his stomach when she said his name. He had no idea she knew who he was.

Just then, her mother noticed that Josie and Jess were talking and beginning to fall behind the group.

"Josephine!" she called. "Keep up now." Slightly disapproving of her talking to what appeared to be a bad boy.

"Well, I've gotta go," Josie said.

"Yeah, this is my turnoff anyway." Jess told her as they approached the old iron gate.

"Is that your shop? Go-Kart Alley?" she asked.

"Yeah, me and my brother got a little business going. We do alright."

"Well if you're ever in Sand Flat, come by Frosty's. My uncle owns it, and I work up there sometimes. Maybe we could go to the water park sometime!"

"Sure!" Jess called as he waved and turned up the backpath.

He had a grin from ear to ear as he drove up to the shop. When he got there he handed the carburetor kit to Brian and went back over to work on frames, whistling.

"What's up with you?" Brian asked, smiling inquisitively.

"Just a great day to be in the go-kart business, that's all," Jess replied.

Chapter 12

Later that week the boys were hard at work trying to get caught up at the shop. They were snowed under with work once again and rarely had time to hang out with the guys. Shawn and John David came by to pry them away from their work.

"Come on, guys!" Shawn pleaded. "You've been working your tails off in here to make sure everyone else has fun during the summer. Don't you think it's time you had a little fun?"

"What are you talking about? This *is* fun for us," Jess said.

"I mean, what could be more fun than working in the most prominent go-kart shop on the trail, and building the best go-karts?"

"Riding them!" John David said.

"We ride all the time," Brian said. "To the junk yard, the parts store, dad's shop…"

"I'm not talking about for work. I'm talking serious riding," John David told them. "I just got word that the gravel pit is on shutdown for a month. There isn't a soul around there. With all that fine crushed gravel, ramps, and pits. We could have a lot of fun."

"Come on, guys, we've all been working hard. We need to have some fun!" Shawn said.

Jess got to thinking about the other day.

"You know, you're right. We do deserve a break. We could do some serious riding in the pits, and maybe head over to Sand Flat for a root beer float. I hear Frosty's has the best around," Jess told them. "Of course, you guys will have to help us get caught up when we get back."

They put all the tools away and tidied up the shop before locking the doors. They were getting their stuff together to go and Jess was getting a Sun-drop for everyone out of the machine.

"Do you think we should take some swim trunks? Sand Flat does have that little water park!" Jess mentioned nonchalantly.

"Yeah!" The others erupted at the idea.

Jess and Brian went into the house to get their swim trunks and an extra pair for Shawn, while John David had a pair with him. A quick call to Roman and some other friends, and they were on their way out to the gravel pit.

The convoy of karts made a turn onto the old road at the end of the drag strip and headed into the pits to do some cutting up. There were paths all through the area lined with finely crushed gravel. The loose road base made it fun to spin the tires and slide around making fish-tail turns. They kicked up a lot of dust and threw a lot of rocks.

Through the course of the morning an agility circuit started to take shape: a path around and through the obstacles, up and down the ramps, in and out if the pits. The boys chased each other around it, and then made it a timed course. Each one taking turns trying to beat the others' time. Jess was still the fastest, but not by much. So, just to make it fair, they gave him a handicap to even things up. The morning was a good time for all.

Covered in dust with all their wild driving demons out, the group of boys decided to head to the water park. They played their usual game of leapfrog along the trail. Sometimes Shawn would be funny and act like he was whipping his kart like a horse to go faster while he passed. They were having a great time as a group of friends that all shared a common sense of life.

As they started to enter Sand Flat, Jess timed it so he was at the back of the line. He did this because Frosty's would be coming up soon, and he wanted to split off from the group for a little bit. When he spotted the silhouette of a root beer mug and burger on the back of the sign, he peeled off the trail and headed to it. He pulled up on a dirt patch between the parking lot and the property line, in view of the service counter. Then he walked over to the door.

His heart was in his throat as he pulled open the door. It almost felt as if he wouldn't be strong enough to open it, but he did. Making his way to the counter, he scanned the restaurant to see if she was there.

"Could I help you?," a man behind the counter asked.

"I'll probably get a float later," Jess replied.

"Could I help you *now*?" the man asked after an awkward pause.

"Oh...uh...Is...uh...Josie here?" Jess finally fumbled out, embarrassed.

"No, she didn't come in today. Sorry," the man said to him.

"Oh...Well, I'll be in later," Jess stammered.

"For a float, right?" The man laughed.

"Uh...Yeah," Jess said, turning to walk out. He felt like running out, because he was acting so dumb. He pushed on the door and started out.

"Wait!" the man called to Jess. "Is that your go-kart?"

"Yes?"

The man pulled a note from by the phone.

"A blue go-kart with silver wheels...Brown hair...Are you Jess?," the man asked.

"Yeah?," Jess said, puzzled.

"Josie called and said if you came in, to call this number," The man said handing a slip of paper to Jess and sliding the phone over the counter.

Nervously, Jess dialed the number and waited for an answer. It rang three times and then...

"Hello?" A young girl's voice came over the line.

"Uh...Is Josie there?," Jess asked.

"Yes. Could I ask who's calling?," The voice said.

"Jess."

He could her the muffle of someone covering the receiver but could still make out...

"It's him!"

"Jess?" Josie's voice came on. Jess got butterflies.

"Hi, it's me," he said.

"Where are you at?," she asked.

"I'm at Frosty's. Listen, me and some friends are going up to the water park, and I thought maybe you might want to meet us?"

"Sure, we weren't doing anything anyway. I'm just hanging out at a friend's house. When are you going?" she asked.

"My friends are probably there already. I'm on my way now."

"Great, we'll see you there," she said before hanging up.

Jess slid the phone back to the man behind the counter and thanked him. He got in his kart and took off for the water park.

The guys were all giving him a hard time trying to figure out where he went.

"This wouldn't have anything to do with me seeing Josie Mayfield riding through town the other day, would it?" John David asked. "You were awfully interested in going to Frosty's."

"You know her?" Jess asked.

"Aha!" John David exclaimed. "I knew it. Her parents are one of my customers and she was asking me about you the other day."

"How does she know about me?" Jess asked him.

"I don't know. Why don't you ask her? There she is," John David said, pointing to her.

She walked up and said hi to John David and then Jess. She introduced her friend, and they all went into the little water park.

Jess had a good time visiting with her and sliding down the slides together. Jess's group was a little out of joint about him spending so much time with her, but they got over it.

They stayed until Josie's friend had to go, and the boys had their fill of swimming. They were all ready for a Frosty's root beer float. So they said goodbye to Josie, and loaded up on their karts and headed to the drive-in on their way home.

When they got there, Jess noticed a familiar go-kart outside, and a familiar face through the window. It was the boy who tried to race him the day he was coming back from Sand Flat with the carburetor kit. On the way to the door, Jess mentioned it to John David.

"That's Tony Patterson," John David told him. "He's Sand

Flat's equivalent of Zack Richter. He's also Josie's boyfriend."

"Boyfriend!" Jess exclaimed.

"Or...was, I guess. I think they broke up," John David said. "Didn't you see him eyeing you up from the baseball field next to the park? He was watching you big time."

"Great. Now you tell me," Jess said woefully.

The boys all ordered floats and paid for them. Then took a seat in one part of the restaurant away from the other group of kids — most of the Sand Flat baseball team that included Tony Patterson.

Jess tried to be cool and act like he didn't know about Tony. Tony kept watching Jess and making comments in his conversation directed for him to overhear. Jess played it off and just waited for everyone to finish so he could get out of there. But, Josie's uncle interrupted the calm.

"Did you get to see Josie?" he asked. "Hello there, John David."

"Yeah. She was there," Jess replied.

"Good. She's a sweet girl. You better be real nice to her." He said walking into the back of the restaurant.

Tony got up and walked up to Jess. Jess saw him coming, so he got up, too. He didn't want a confrontation sitting down, with Tony standing over him.

"You stay away from Josie! She's *my* girlfriend," Tony said, low and mean like.

"Well, she has never mentioned having a boyfriend to me," Jess told him, standing his ground.

"Well, she does. And you better stay away from her. Matter of fact, you better stay away from Sand Flat all together," Tony threatened.

"Maybe I should just stay away from you," Jess said, but suddenly wished he hadn't. It didn't come out like he thought it would, and the baseball players were all laughing at him.

"Yeah...that too," Tony said laughing.

Jess was infuriated and embarrassed all at the same time. Just then, Brian came up to Tony.

"Stay away from you 'cause you stink!" Brian said, trying to help out his brother but only making it worse.

"Shut up you little twerp!," Tony said, turning to Brian. Then he gave Brian a shove that knocked him down. Brian started to cry.

Tony was laughing about that too as he turned back to Jess, just in time to catch a full right-handed blow to the mouth.

Jess was an extremely nice guy, but there was nothing in the world that would set him off quicker than someone messing with his little brother. The previous situation over the girl just added to the fire.

Jess gave Tony that full-force blow, followed by another quick right. Then he pulled a roundhouse left to Tony's jaw. Tony spun to the left blow and fell down.

Immediately the whole team was up to get Jess, and the Sumner crew was up to defend him. Jess just kept swinging at every baseball jersey he saw. It was an all-out brawl. The athletes outnumbered the country boys, but the country boys were putting up a good fight. They kept swinging until they had the baseball players down, then turned and ran for the door.

Shortly the baseball team was up and coming after them. Unaware that there would be a getaway, the boys had parked kind of far away, unlike the baseball team. They ran clear across the parking lot and hurried for their go-karts. The team was behind them now, all carrying baseball bats.

With a blur of starter cords being pulled and dust flying, the Sumner boys were hightailing it for the trail. The baseball team ran back for their go-karts to follow.

Down the trail, Jess and the others kept looking back to see if they were coming, but never saw them. Jess wondered if Josie's uncle had stopped them, or if maybe they planned revenge later. Either way, he wasn't gonna stop until he was back at his shop.

That night, the boys decided to camp out by the Sumner Creek Bridge, in case the Sand Flat baseball players decided to make a nighttime raid on Sumner. Sitting around the fire, the boys were trying to decide why it was that they were not followed out of Frosty's.

It was then that Brian revealed what he had done. While

the older boys were fighting it out with the ballplayers, he snuck out and sabotaged their go-karts. He had taken a hammer out of his toolbox, and busted off all of the team's spark plugs.

"Oh, great!" Jess said. "They'll be after us for sure now."

Chapter 13

That weekend, the boys continued to take it easy for a little while and work on some of their own projects. Brian spent a good deal of effort in finishing his Yazoo Dragster. He wanted it to shine brightly for the Sumner Fourth of July Parade. Just about all of the go-karts around were being washed and waxed and shined up to be shown off.

Jess was making plans to put some signs on the trailer and pull it through the parade for advertisement. But he was torn, because he didn't want to pull it behind the Heatseeker, and he didn't want to drive the Orange Krate. He finally talked John David into pulling it, and proceeded to get the Heatseeker ready.

Tuesday morning at breakfast, I told the boys to come down to my shop when they got a chance. I had a business proposition I wanted to discuss with them. So they arrived on their karts shortly after I did.

We walked out to the junk area behind the shop. Upon rounding the corner of the building, they saw immediately what I had in mind. Sitting there in a dilapidated heap was a worn-out old industrial buggy.

"We've been installing some machinery at a big plastics plant in Prichard. When I pulled around back of the maintenance department, it was just sitting there with a bunch of junk to be thrown out. I figured you guys might have a use for her...much junk as I see you hauling up and down the trail on your trailer," I told them.

It was a cute little buggy, even if it was worn out. It resembled a miniature flatbed straight truck. There was a bench seat for two atop the steer axle, with control pedals in the floorboards that hung out in front. It had a metal front that protected the passenger and driver's feet that looked like the front of a cabover truck.

The flatbed part was about 6 feet long and covered the back wheels. An overhead rack was built to be able to haul longer lengths of materials up above. Its mismatched green paint, two flat tires and rotten wood bed made it look pretty sad.

"They were using it as a maintenance buggy to carry tools around the plant. Then they used it for outside maintenance work. I guess they got a more suitable replacement, because they just abandoned her," I said.

"Is it electric?," Jess asked.

"No. Come here and look. It has a 10-horse Kohler on it. Natural gas, though, so they could use it indoors. That's no problem to change over, if you don't want to mess with filling the tank. I'm sure Harvey has a carburetor that will fit it. The change over to gasoline isn't much harder than that," I said.

The boys agreed they could use the buggy. Jess even suggested that if they worked hard, they could have it running and painted in time to drive in the parade on Friday.

We got the forklift and loaded it onto a trailer that I used to carry it to the house. The boys met me back at their shop, and we got it unloaded and put in the shed. I left them to their work, which they dove into immediately.

Jess busted out the rotten plywood floor and put it in the burn barrel. Brian moved in to get a good look at the 10-horse. He found the information he needed and was off to the junkyard to get a carburetor.

Jess had the motor on the bench by the time he got back, so he could go straight to work putting his magic touch on it. Jess continued to strip the buggy down to the basics and give it a good looking over.

There were many places that needed welding or straightening, so he fixed them as needed. Upon close examination, Jess found that it was originally an electric cart, and someone had added the natural gas burning engine.

"They must have done this after they started using it outside," Jess told Brian, "because they would have never needed a transmission like this inside the plant."

His examination of the transmission yielded that it was a four-speed with a reverse. The fourth gear was a high-speed one and would come in handy on the trail. Jess had been leery that it would go too slow. The low gear would be powerful enough to start off with a large load.

Jess did all of the metal work to the frame that needed to be done. There was no need to add a hitch for the trailer, because one already existed. The frame was ready to sandblast and paint.

While Brian still worked on the motor, Jess took off the wheels, broke the tires off the flat ones and patched the tubes inside. Then he decided to break down all four tires in order to blast off all of the layers of flat black paint caked on the rims.

Firing up the sandblaster, Jess cleaned away the ugly from the frame and wheels in preparation to paint. He worked a good part of Tuesday and part of Wednesday getting the frame ready. Brian had the engine purring like a kitten, just in time to put the whole rig back together again.

It was a sweet looking little truck when they finished. It was the perfect truck for their business. Painted gloss black with a few chrome accents that they added to look like the big rigs, the little go-kart truck rolled out onto the trail with both boys riding in front.

They took it down to show John David. He then rode on the back of the truck, with them up to Fred's to catch Roman. They needed Roman to come out and detail the paint and add the Go-Kart Alley logo and lettering. He got on it right away and, by Thursday, it was ready for the parade.

For the rest of that day, the boys had to make up for lost time from working on their own projects. Most of the work in the shop had to be out by the Fourth, because everyone wanted their go-karts for the parade.

They practically had to pull an all-nighter, but they finally managed to get out all the work they had promised by the Fourth. They were not tired though, because the Fourth of July Parade was such a big deal every year that their excitement kept them going.

By nine o'clock Friday morning, they had received a substantial amount of money form their jobs and were getting their stuff ready to take to the start of the parade route. Brian decided he wanted to drive the new truck so he loaded the Yazoo Dragster onto the back and pulled the trailer carrying the Orange Krate behind. The truck and trailer were streaming with red, white and blue crepe paper.

Down at the schoolyard where the busses park, the boys took their place in the lineup waiting to start the parade. There were go-karts everywhere, and the parade coordinator had a hard time deciding where to put them all. It was really cool, because most of Jess and Brian's customers had made signs and put them on their go-karts which read "Customized by Go-Kart Alley."

Waiting in line Jess noticed a buddy a few rows over whom he had rarely seen all summer. It was his friend who started the rock band. The guys had their instruments set up on a four-wheeled haywagon pulled by a tractor. There was a generator on the front of the wagon to power their. A sign on both sides of the wagon read "Engine Joe--Music To Speed To."

The band had played at Fred's a couple of times, but Jess hadn't gotten a chance to see them yet and didn't know what they sounded like. So he walked over before the parade started to say "Hi." His buddy was glad to see him and gave him a homemade tape of their music.

As the floats started to move, Jess thanked him for the tape and returned to his kart. The band was a considerable distance ahead of Jess, so he still didn't get to hear them live. But as Jess and Brian's line started to move, Jess popped in the tape of his friend's band. It was lively, good music. If you had to put a label on it I suppose it would be called rock music, but it was country tinged with raw punk energy. Jess liked it a lot. It came as no surprise that, since their motive to start a band was go-karts, most of their songs were about go-karts.

The go-karts along the parade all moved in a sort of formation. Generally in groups of four or five, they made figure eights around two floats. They had to keep a close eye out for kids darting out for candy. The go-kart truck counted as a float so Jess, John David, Shawn and Roman all circled around it and the FFA float. Jess was having a blast speeding around in the street blaring his buddy's music.

At the end of the parade, there is always a big festival in the park with a few rides and a lot of food and games. The guys all found a safe place to park their karts and went out to enjoy the festival.

Later in the evening, Engine Joe set up to play on their hay wagon in the baseball field. Jess was now a big fan and came out to dance under the moonlight along with tons of other kids there from the go-karting scene.

Chapter 14

The Monday after the Fourth, things were back to normal around the boy's shop, and business was back up after their advertising in the parade. They were hard at work making more go-karts run. It was pretty quiet except for the music of ratchet wrenches, welders and, of course, Engine Joe on the tape player.

The area behind their shop looked like a miniature used car lot. There were new and used go-karts, for sale or trade, all over the place, lined up in neat rows. There were one seaters and two seaters and frames with no motors. Some were taken in trade where they would sell them as is in a day or two at a profit. The old frames they put little work into, threw on an old, but running motor and made a better profit on. Some karts were just there for sale on consignment for other kids.

Little piles were here and there of things that they hauled back from the junkpiles. Wheels and tires, tubing, steering wheels — all sorts of stuff someone might want on their go-kart. It was a regular swap meet at Go-Kart Alley.

The calm working environment that morning was suddenly interrupted when a frantic kid, panting and out of breath, came running into the shop.

"You guys! You gotta help me!," he gasped. "I was riding my brothers go-kart. He's away at camp, and he never lets me ride it but I took it out anyway since he won't be back till tomorrow!"

"Catch your breath, dude!," Jess told him.

The kid just kept on. "So I was riding the trail and I somehow went too far and ended up in Sumner and then I saw this old road so I decided to take it! And it led back into these pits and trails where there was all this construction equipment!"

"The gravel pits?," Jess asked.

"Yeah I guess. So it was really cool and I was riding around all these trails and stuff and I was getting pretty good so I started going faster on them but I guess I got too fast because I tried to slow down but the throttle hung and I lost control through an "S" curve and hit a crane. Now it's all messed up and you gotta help me!" He finished, almost passing out.

"So you came too fast through the piles and plowed into the tracks of the dragline. I told you guys that was the trickiest spot on that course." Jess spoke to the kid and then to Brian. "So where is your brother's kart?"

"It's still down there, or I hope it still is. It's stuck to the crane, if no one stole it yet," the kid said.

"Well, we better take a look. Help me carry this toolbox." Jess said to the boy.

They carried a toolbox out and threw it onto the back of the little truck. Jess grabbed a cable with hooks on the ends and threw it on as well. He got in the driver's seat and motioned for the kid to load up in the passenger seat.

As they started down the backpath to the trail, Jess looked over at the worried kid.

"What's your name?" Jess asked.

"Chris," he replied. "But my friends all call me Topher."

"Well, Topher, you can calm down. We'll get your brother's kart out OK," Jess told him.

"I hope so. He's gonna kill me," Topher said.

Jess turned out onto the trail and headed for the gravel pit road. At the end of the dragstrip he turned off the trail and snaked the little truck back in the brush-grown gravel pit road. Jess knew exactly where Topher had wrecked and drove straight to it.

They pulled around the piles to see a slick-looking light blue go-kart with white pinstripes, crunched up into the tracks of the dragline. Jess killed the motor and Chris walked directly over to the kart and regained his worried look.

"Oh my God...It's worse than I remember. He's gonna kill me...He's gonna kill me!," Topher said.

"You did smuck her up pretty good," Jess said calmly. "But he's not gonna kill you. When Brian and I get done with her, He'll never know it happened."

"Easy for you to say. You don't know how much time he

spends just looking this thing over each day. He'll notice. I
know he will. I just don't think you can pull it off," he told
Jess.

"Well, I don't care, I'll fix it just the same. He's sure gonna
kill you, if you bring it home like that," Jess told him.

Jess backed the truck around and lined it up with the go-
kart. He took the cable and fastened one end onto the truck's
hitch and the other onto the go-kart frame. He pulled ahead
until the cable was taut and then let out the clutch to give the
kart a good swift tug. The go-kart popped free from the
dragline instantly.

Topher helped Jess load the kart up onto the truck. They
climbed back on and headed back to the shop. Brian greeted
them as soon as they pulled into the shop. The Go-Kart Alley
boys went to work like doctors in an emergency room as the
victim's family hovered nervously around.

They worked as long as they could stand it with Topher
buzzing about. Finally Jess and Brian took a break. When
they did, Topher stayed inside and started to work on the kart
himself.

They couldn't have this. Jess quickly hatched a plan to get
rid of him while they finished the emergency job.

"Hey, Topher!" Jess called inside. "Did you plan to pay up
front?"

"Um…I don't know. I thought I would wait and see how
you do," Topher said.

"Well, regardless of how we do, a job like this will still cost
at least $40. We'll probably need some parts and paint, so it's
best if you pay up front."

"Forty dollars! I don't have that kind of money," he said.

"Well, what do you have? We'll haul it to your house now
for five bucks," Jess told him.

"No…I can't have that. I can get the money. Do you really
need it up front?" Topher asked.

"Well, I'll tell you what. I know you're not from around
here, so I'll cut you a break. I'll let you take that old junker
over there for tonight. Does your brother keep his kart under
a tarp?"

"Yeah?" Topher told him.

"Good. Take that one, and put it under the tarp. That will keep your parents from finding out. Then you break into your piggy bank, and bring the money first thing in the morning. I trust you'll come back, else I get the better end of the deal by keeping your brother's kart. And you don't want that. Right?" Jess told him.

"Will it really be $40?" Topher asked.

"Maybe not. But you'd better bring the whole amount just in case we run into problems."

Topher finally agreed to the plan and left on the junker. Jess and Brian were able to return to work in peace.

By the end of the night, Jess had fixed all of the framework and the broken wheel. The flywheel key had been sheared when the motor came to a sudden halt during the impact. Brian replaced that and had it running in no time. By early morning the paint was dry, and Roman came out to match up the pinstripes.

At nine o'clock, Topher came rattling up the backpath on the old junker to see his brother's go-kart glistening in the sun, good as new.

"Your bill comes to twenty-five-fifty," Jess told him, as he gave the repaired go-kart a good looking over.

"Man. You guys weren't kidding. You really did fix it all up. I can't even tell where it was wrecked!," Topher said in astonishment.

He paid his bill, thanked the boys, and drove off in a hurry to get it back under the tarp before his brother got home from camp.

With that episode over, once again they returned to their normal grind at the shop.

The next day a delivery had to be made, of a brand new go-kart they had just built from scratch, to a rich kid from Sand Flat. Jess was all too eager to head eastward on the trail. Brian knew why and just rolled his eyes.

This go-kart, cherry red and tricked out real good, had already been built once, but the rich kid who ordered it, left on vacation for two weeks. A kid named Billy, from Pritchard, heard about Go-Kart Alley and came down to check out the shop. He fell in love with the new go-kart and blew his life savings on it. They built this second one and had it finished just in time for the rich kid's return from vacation.

They were going to make a lot of money off these two go-karts. Jess loaded up the new kart on the truck and headed on his way. His first stop was not the go-kart's new home, but Frosty's. There he found Josie working the counter.

"Hey, there! Is the Root beer here as sweet as you?" Jess said in a dorky voice, being funny.

Josie laughed. "What are you doing here?"

"I had to deliver a kart we built for a kid here in town," he told her.

"What are you doing after that?," she asked.

"Then I gotta get back to the shop. We're kinda behind right now. Why?"

"It's just kinda slow here today, and I thought maybe you might want to go back to the water park or something."

"I wish I could, but Brian needs me. And besides, baseball practice will be over soon, and I don't think I can take on the whole team by myself," Jess told her.

"Yeah, I heard about that. I don't think you have to worry about that any. Their coach got pretty mad at them for fighting in public. And as far as Tony, I'm sorry about him. He's just a big jerk who thinks he's my boyfriend. I hear he's afraid to face you by himself. They say you whooped him pretty good."

Jess smiled at what she had to say.

"Well, if you're not doing anything, you could ride with me on this delivery. Then I could take you back and show you our shop. I'll have you back in plenty of time for supper. What do you say?"

She thought it sounded like fun, so she told her uncle "Goodbye" and went out with Jess onto the truck.

Jess made his delivery to a satisfied customer and collected his pay. Then he made his way onto the trail and headed back to the shop. Brian was slightly annoyed to see that he actually brought her back to the shop. But it wasn't long before Brian was acting goofy around her and halfway flirting himself.

Josie was very impressed with all that Jess and Brian knew how to do. Jess set her up with a stool to sit on while she watched him work. He gave her an extra welding helmet to put on, so she didn't burn her eyes while watching him weld.

She sat for a while and then wandered about, admiring all of the handiwork in the shop. Watching Brian work his magic on the motors for a while, she paid him a big compliment on how professional and thorough he was at his work. He was beginning to like her more and more.

She finally made a comment about the music playing in the shop.

"Who is this?," She asked.

"Oh, that's a friend of mine's band from Sumner. Do you like them?" Jess asked.

"They are really good! What's their name?"

"Engine Joe."

"Really? My uncle just booked them to play at Frosty's tomorrow night. You guys should come out to see them."

"That sounds like fun. I haven't gotten to see them play a serious gig yet. What time?"

She told him all about the gig, and he agreed to be there early enough to spend some time with her. Then he called all his buddies to get them to come.

It was all set up for Thursday night. The Sumner gang would be there in support of their favorite local band.

When it started getting late, Jess drove Josie down to get some pizza at Fred's and drove her back to Sand Flat. On the way they pulled off by the lake to talk for a while. She told him how impressive it was that he and his brother had their own business. She forecasted great things in the future for a boy as bright and talented as Jess. He told her how nice it was to meet a girl that cared a little more about things that were important, rather than hair and makeup, or who was in the "in" crowd.

When they couldn't stay any longer without making Josie late, Jess started up the truck and drove her on home. He drove back to the shop that night on cloud nine. When he got there, Brian finally had to admit that she was a pretty cool girl.

Chapter 15

The next afternoon, they got things wrapped up early at the shop. John David and Shawn were there, and they were waiting on a bunch more to go with them. When everyone had assembled, they sped off down the backpath on their way to Frosty's.

When they got there, Engine Joe's equipment was already set up on a little, temporary stage in the back of the seating area. Jess recognized the drum set and the little toolbox his friend kept his guitar accessories in. He saw Josie right away and went over to say "Hi." She wasn't working that night, so they ordered some food and got a booth together. John David and Brian sat with them, too, but they didn't mind. It was good company and made for good conversation.

They ate their food and talked while waiting for the band to take the stage. The drummer, bass player and one guitar player had shown up but Jess's friend, the lead singer and guitar player, was not anywhere to be seen. It was probably his gimmick to be fashionably late.

The wait wasn't bothering Jess any; it gave him more time to talk with Josie. He invited her to come over by the games, where they played a few good games of pinball with Jess running one flipper and Josie running the other. They split a double cherry sour for dessert and, finally, Jess saw his friend come through the door. Jess gave a little wave and said "Hi" as he made his way to the stage.

The young man was dressed in a black T-shirt and loose-fitting worn blue jeans, adorned with a trucker's wallet and chrome chain. With a shaggy, unkempt mop of black hair, the boy took the stage. He picked up his guitar and put the strap over his head. Turning it on, he strummed a few chords, and then went through the strings one at a time, checking to see if they were in tune. He twisted a knob or two and went through the strings once more. Another few chords and he was satisfied with his tuning and stepped up to the microphone.

"Hey-Hey. Ho-Ho." He said into the mike, testing the sound. He turned around to check the meters and adjust some knobs on the towers of speakers, then stepped back up to the mike.

"Evenin', everybody. We're Engine Joe. Thanks for being here!" he said as the crowd began to cheer. "Two—Three--Four!"

And the band smashed into their opening song. It was "Good Times," by Nobody's Children but with the words changed around to be about the trail and go-karts.

"Well I work all day from nine to five
Tryin to make enough to keep my motor alive.
When five o'clock comes I try to drive to the swimmin' hole.
That's when I find out I got a cracked sediment bowl.
Go-karts! Yeah, go-karts."

When the song ended the crowd erupted into applause, cheering and whistling. Engine Joe really made a big hit, and Jess was proud to be able to say that he knew them. As the crowd cheered, the singer spoke into the mike.

"Thanks a lot. Thanks," he said, and soon began another song.

Song after song they played, wowing the audience with their talent. When the band had finished their third encore, it was pretty late, and the Sumner gang had to drive home in the dark. Luckily, a few of the guys had flashlights or spotlights to aid finding their way home. Several of them were bound to be in trouble when they got home, for staying out so late. Jess said "Goodbye" to the band and bragged on what a good job they had done. Being modest as usual, Jess's friend thanked him for coming out. He said "Goodbye" to Josie, and the boys were headed for home.

The next day, Jess couldn't get the images out of his head of the good time he had the night before. The songs of the lively band echoed in his ears in a way different from the tape he had listened to over and over again. There was something about a live show that just made the music better. Jess tried to remember bits and pieces of the new songs that weren't on the tape. He managed to get out a word or two of the refrain but ended up just humming the rest.

Work rocked on pretty regular, again at the shop. They were getting caught up to the point that they were almost bored. The boys found more time to hang out now and spent more time with friends. They were at Fred's every day and, sometimes, two or three times a day.

The trail hummed with the sound of go-karts putting up and down the way. Everyone was busy tooling around, doing some work, but a lot of playing. Jess and Brian had been in the go-kart business for a little over five weeks now and full-time for a month.

They had managed to put just about everybody that wanted one, in a go-kart and managed fixed up the rest of them. Most of the kids were starting to learn more about maintenance and were even fixing their own problems now. They only stopped in to ask advice from Jess and Brian. So a lot of Go-Kart Alley's work was done right from Fred's parking lot.

Wednesday of that week, everything was pretty normal and Jess had been feeling good hanging out with his friends but suddenly got a sick feeling in the pit of his stomach. This came when he saw someone that he hadn't seen in a while. It was one of Zack Patterson's little toadies. No one else paid any attention, and it probably didn't mean anything, but it bothered Jess just the same.

He had just come in and sat with some friends and ate like nothing was up. Jess convinced himself that he was just overreacting and went back to having a good time. It wasn't until the boy was leaving the restaurant when that feeling returned to Jess. As he was walking to the door, he stopped and turned around. Jess was watching him closely. He turned to look directly at Jess and grinned real big. Then he pulled open the door and left.

Suddenly, Jess had lost his appetite and quit contributing to the conversation. When they left Fred's, Jess went back to the shop and did some tuning up on his go-kart. He changed the belts on his transmission and cleaned the air filter. That afternoon, the spark plug was changed, a new set of ignition points added and he put some special high-octane gas in the gas tank. Jess didn't know what he was getting ready for, but he thought he ought to be ready for it.

Late that afternoon the gang was back up at Fred's to hang out again. Jess had that feeling again when he showed up, but it went away as soon as he got inside and everything seemed normal enough. The pizza was as good as ever and the Sundrop was ice cold in the bottle. And, as usual, the topic of conversation at Jess's table was go-karts.

Engine Joe wasn't there but, through some crafty engineering, they were being played on the jukebox. The band had found an old, old-record copying machine designed for duplicating 78-rpm records. They made a few changes to it and were able to get their music from tape to 45-rpm record, which is what the jukebox played.

The music was playing, and the place almost roared with kids talking and laughing. Jess kept an occasional eye on the trail but was very much having a good time. He and his friends continued to tease one another and swap stories. Soon John David made a comment.

"Who's cutting trees at this time of day," he said.

"What are you talking about?," Jess said in a half laugh.

"You don't hear that? It's a chainsaw, and it's getting closer."

Jess swallowed and looked to the trail. When he did, "it" rounded the corner into Fred's. It was a go-kart, with Zack at the wheel. Following him were all his toadies.

It was hard to tell if it was Zack's same go-kart, because it was covered by a fiberglass body in the style of a Corvette. As it pulled up in front of the doors, you could see the glass body was chopped to fit two chainsaw engines in the rear. The body was one of those commonly seen on a go-kart some store was giving away in a raffle, with a soda company logo or something on it.

It didn't have any logo on it now. The fiberglass body had been repainted black and covered in red airbrushed paintings of skulls, demons with horns, flames, and even half-naked women. The disturbing paint job was covered in a clearcoat gloss so thick, the graphics almost looked three-dimensional.

Squeaking to a prompt halt, the engines whined down to a high, noisy
idle. Zack's buddies were scrambling to get parked and follow him. Zack jumped up from his kart and hustled through the door into the pizza restaurant.

The back room was in a hush in anticipation of what was going to happen. The only sound was a video game waiting to be played and Engine Joe on the jukebox. All of Zack's gang made it in the door.

"Let's see what your piece of crap, old man, junkyard kart can do now, Mr. 'Go-Kart Alley'!," Zack said, with an antsy grin.

Jess looked past him at the twin engines on the go-kart outside. As he had been learning more about go-karts, he had heard stories about go-kart racing as far back as the fifties. He was finding out that the kind of karting the kids had been doing that summer on the trail was almost primitive compared to what adult racers had done 25 years earlier. Brian had discovered that a bigger engine didn't always mean a faster go-kart, and that finesse was the key. Jess knew there would come a day when the Heatseeker wouldn't be the fastest on the trail, but he didn't know it would be this day. He thought he still had time to prepare.

Looking at the engines, Jess recognized them to be a popular combination back in the day. They were two 10-horse McCullough chainsaw engines. Two-cycle engines that gained all of their horsepower from high rpm's. Jess knew it was a powerful combination, and the Heatseeker hardly stood a chance.

"Come on, Jess. You can take him!," everyone was saying.

Jess had nothing to say, he just pushed his way past Zack and out the door, still carrying his bottle of Sun-drop. He got in the Heatseeker, put the bottle in its holder and fired up the motor. Zack and his gang took off for the drag strip. As Jess pulled out to follow, everyone from the restaurant was running out to their go-karts. This was a major, unanticipated race by the two competitors who had started "go-kart fever" on the trail. Nobody wanted to miss this.

Zack was on the line when Jess got there. All the others were pulling off to park and scrambling to get a good place to watch. Zack wanted plenty of people watching, so he gave a glance to his buddy to wait before flagging the race off.

When everyone had arrived, he nodded to the flagman who stepped out in front of the two karts. Jess worriedly looked over at Zack, who grinned largely staring straight ahead. Jess revved his engine and gripped the wheel. He tried to convince himself that Zack didn't know enough to pull it off. He may have added the engines, the body and got some thug to paint it, but Zack didn't have enough practical experience to make those engines work to their full capability. There was no way Zack was gonna beat Jess at karting. It just couldn't happen.

As the flagman stiffened his arm and began the count, Jess winced and waited for the go. When it came, Jess punched the gas. First gear took hold beautifully with the new belts. The Harvey-built Kohler engine was quickly gaining on redline, and Jess was getting ready to shift. He had a commanding lead on Zack right off the line.

There was always a slight sluggish period when he first hit second gear, but the motor quickly pulled out of it. Jess noticed that Zack had gained a little during that time but could feel the Heatseeker pulling away again and had a good feeling. The engine was winding up towards top speed again in second gear, and Jess felt it would only be a short time before he would win the race.

Against Jess' plan, Zack kept gaining, and was doing it faster now than before. It seemed that the chainsaw engines had low starting torque but, once they got going, the rpm's multiplied like wildfire. Zack was beside Jess three-quarters of the way through the race and flashed a smile at him as he kept going past.

Jess stared at the glowing eyes of one of the comic book paintings on the rear of Zack's kart as it sped past him on to victory. In disbelief, Jess couldn't take his eyes off the go-kart.

He noticed a movement out of the corner of his eye and

focused his attention back on his lane. To his surprise, a small boulder about one foot in diameter was rolling down the steep embankment of the railroad bed from above. By the time Jess noticed it and realized what it was, it was already in his lane. He started to swerve, but there was no time. The go-kart plowed into the rock with the front right corner of the sheet-metal body.

BANG! It hit, smashing in the sheet metal and making solid contact with the frame. Jess felt a solid jar at his right foot, and the kart made a quick jerk to the left. The blow to the front end by the boulder had bent the tie-rods to the steering and the kart reacted as if Jess had made a sharp left turn at full throttle.

Unable to control it, Jess was quickly carried off the left side of the trail, where the steep embankment continued down. The hillside was lined with young sapling trees and brush. Jess braced for the jar of hitting one of the trees, but it never came. The go-kart careened over the edge without hitting an obstacle.

The rough terrain and steep slope made it impossible for the go-kart to remain upright, and it began to flip. It started rolling sideways at first and then made a transition to end over end, crashing and smashing its way down the hillside.

Jess's friends watched in horror as the twisted mess of kart rolled it's way towards the bottom where a tributary of Sumner Creek lay at the foot of the hill. In fear of the terrible mess ending up in the creek, John David ran to help his friend before it came to a stop. When it finally did, the front half of the kart was upside down in the water. Jess could feel that his feet were wet.

Dazed for a little bit, he shook his head and got his bearing. The only sound was a little trickle of water in the creek and the faint noise of the crowd coming to his rescue. A very audible "Psssss — Psssss — Psssss" then interrupted the calm after the wreck.

At first Jess figured his bottle of Sun-drop had somehow gotten upset in the rolling and was leaking on the hot muffler. The sight of green, broken glass all around him proved that wrong. He soberly came to full attention when he realized the smell all around him.

It was gasoline! And Jess was covered in it. If that gas dripping on the muffler ignited, it would be a very bad thing.

Jess quickly unbuckled the safety belt he was wearing and crawled out between the soft mud of the creek bed and twisted metal body. The roll bar behind his head kept the body just enough off the ground to get out.

Shortly after he was out and making his way up the slope to get away from it, the Heatseeker burst into flames. John David and the others making their way down the slope stopped and gasped at the sight of the fire. When they saw the movement of Jess free of the wreckage, they continued on to his aid.

Some ran to Jess to make sure he was all right. The rest ran to the creek, splashing water on the flaming wreckage to put out the fire. When the fire was out, Jess and his rescuers made their way up the embankment as dozens of spectators watched from above.

On level ground, Jess was walking around fine. He was not injured during the wreck that he could tell. Only a few possible bruises and scratches. The worst injury of all was his broken spirit. Not only did he lose the race, but his go-kart was demolished.

Zack drove up, gave a nod and a grunt to the fact that Jess was all right, and drove away. He and his buddies congregated at the race start line and then left.

"That's funny," John David said. "I don't remember Tony coming out with Zack and his bunch."

Jess looked down at the group of go-karts leaving and saw the black kart that he had raced in Sand Flat leaving with Zack's bunch. He dismissed any ideas he was having and looked back down at his wrecked go-kart, shaking his head.

"Come on. Let's get this cleaned up," Shawn said.

"I'll go get the truck and some cable," Brian said.

Shawn, John David and Roman stayed to console Jess and help boost his ego, while Brian went to get the truck. They were trying everything to get him to cheer up, but with no success.

"You didn't paint that for him, did you?" Jess said to Roman.

"No, man. I wouldn't do that to you. I don't know where he got that done. It looks like one of those weirded-out high school kids' work to me," Roman said.

"Good," Jess grunted, and went back to being silent.

Chapter 16

When Brian got back with the truck, the boys went to work fishing the wreckage up from the creek below. There was only so much cable, so they had to drag it little by little up the steep slope until it was close enough to pull up with the truck. They finally got it up on the trail and loaded onto the truck.

It was a sad sight. There wasn't a single place on it that wasn't dented, bent or twisted. The paint was black and burnt over half of the go-kart, and the rest was scratched and peeling around the creases.

Jess hopped on the truck with Brian, and they drove back to the shop. There they were looking it over closely and assessing the damage. There was still oil leaking out of the crankcase, which brought Jess's attention to more damage.

"Well, let's get her off," Jess told the guys.

"Don't you want to pull it a little closer to the shop first?," John David asked. "So we can get her in there and get to work fixing her up again."

"Are you kidding, this thing's junk. Look at it. All bent up, the block is busted, wheels broken, transmission ruined. It's shot. Might as well start all over. Besides, it wouldn't be able to beat anything, anyway. My day has come. You can't just upgrade to a bigger motor to win anymore. I don't care if it just sits here and rots--I'm goin' to the house," Jess told them woefully, and then walked away without even unloading his old go-kart.

Brian and the other guys went ahead and unloaded it and set it close to the wall behind the shop, covering it with a ratty old tarp. Not knowing what to do about their friend and brother, they decided to let him have some space for a while.

The next morning, Jess caught me at breakfast and asked if I needed any help at my shop. I told him I could always use his help.

"But what about your go-kart business?," I asked him.

"Aw, we're starting to run out of work. And besides, I was getting pretty tired of it anyway," he told me.

I was a little disheartened by his loss of interest in the business I was so proud of him for starting. But I told him he was welcome to work for me anytime and offered more money like I had promised.

"I don't care about the money. I just want something to keep me busy," he said, and we went out to the truck to go to work.

When we got to the shop, I lined out a job for him on the CNC milling machine. It was an easy job, because it was already set up. All he would have to do was bolt down some castings and punch the cycle start button.

"Load 'em up and punch 'em off. Green button, go," I told him.

He went right to work. He changed the parts speedily after each cycle of the machine and finished the job ahead of schedule. When he did, he came to me for more work.

I put a more experienced hand on the machine to set up on a new job and found some work in shipping and receiving for Jess. It was boxing up parts to send out to be plated. One box had to be built for chrome plating, and one for copper. He buried himself in the job and worked steadily until he had the parts ready to ship off.

When that was done, I had him reading blueprints and laying out materials and tools for all of the jobs that we would be starting soon. That took up most of the day until about two o'clock. Then I put him back in shipping and receiving to check in some castings that were just delivered.

"This is a new casting company we are dealing with, and they have been sending us a lot of junk. Here's a good example of what we want," I said, showing him our model casting. "Check every one thoroughly to make sure there are no imperfections."

Jess worked at that until it was time to go home. When I had second shift lined out and going, we drove home. On the way, I could tell something was bothering Jess, but I didn't know how to figure out what. I decided maybe he was just having a bad day or something, so I just didn't say anything.

The next day there was a slack period, so I brought Jess in

the office and trained him some on the computer. We had a state-of-the-art computer-aided drafting system, and I was making some blueprints on it. He picked up on it right away and was able to do some simple drawings. Once he got the hang of it, I turned him loose to make some updated copies of blueprints that we had been using so long that they were falling apart.

He worked at that most of the day, until I needed him to get all of the flawed castings ready to send back to the foundry we had gotten them from. He crated them all up and checked the paperwork to see that we had the correct amount of good castings still out of the box.

The next day, a new machine we were purchasing needed to be picked up in Bay City. Just to get out of the shop, I volunteered to go get it myself. I asked Jess to go along with me in our old cabover Freightliner semi-truck and flatbed trailer. We fueled up, checked the air pressure in the tires and that all the lights were working. We grabbed a healthy breakfast of chocolate milk and donuts from the convenience store and, by seven o'clock that morning as the sun was shining golden over the trees, the old truck roared out onto the highway.

"Old Red sure is loud!," Jess exclaimed to me, over the roar of the diesel engine.

"Yeah! But this old Detroit sure has been a good one," I said.

"Detroit? I thought Red was a Freightliner."

"He is. But, the engine is a Detroit. They call it that because it's made by General Motors, the car company. And since it was the only major diesel engine to come from a car company based in Detroit, it got the name Detroit," I said.

"Are they all this loud, or is it just because it's old?" Jess asked.

"They're loud like that because they're a two-cycle engine instead of a four, like most diesel engines."

"Like a go-kart engine is a four-stroke right?," Jess asked.

"Yeah. Four-stroke or four-cycle. But two-cycle is like a chainsaw or a weed eater. They fire every time the piston comes to the top."

"Then when does it intake and exhaust?"

"Well, it does that on the power stroke, sort of. See, there are holes in the sides of the cylinders near bottom dead center called ports. As the piston is coming down, it comes past these ports. When the piston is all the way down, these holes are all the way open. Fresh air and fuel come in from one side, pushing exhaust gases out the other. Make sense?," I asked.

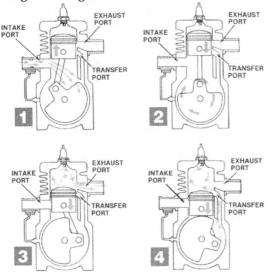

"I guess. But what *makes* the fresh and fuel come in?," he asked.

"When the piston goes up, it draws a mixture of fresh air and fuel through the carburetor and into the crankcase. When it comes back down, it squeezes that fuel-air mixture in the crankcase and forces it into the cylinder through a transfer port.," I told him.

"That makes sense," he said. "But how can there be fuel-air in the crankcase full of oil?"

"There's no oil in the crankcase of a two cycle. That's why you have to add two cycle oil to weed eater gas. It's what actually lubricates the crankcase."

"But I saw you put oil in the crankcase of the Detroit this morning," He said.

"Well, that what I told you was more for chainsaws and weed eaters. The Detroit diesel is different because *it* doesn't draw air into the crankcase. There's a compressor called a blower that forces fresh air in through inlet ports. What happens is, when the piston goes down past the inlet ports, regular exhaust valves open in the head to let the exhaust gasses out. As the piston comes back up on the compression stroke, the exhaust valves and inlet ports all close. At top dead center, an injector squirts a spray of diesel fuel into the cylinder which ignites just by the heat of the compressed air inside and kicks off the power stroke"

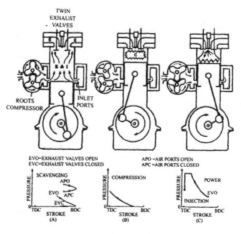

"That seems kinda simple for an engine," Jess said.

"Yeah, and the beauty of it is, you can add as many cylinders as you want for more power, and each can use the same components. Because each piston fires each time it comes to the top, it's like getting twice the power."

"That's pretty cool," he said.

When we got to Bay City, they were waiting to load our machine. Inside of an hour, we were on our way back to the shop. When we got there, we promptly unloaded the machine and started setting it up. I parked Old Red in its shed.

Jess helped set up the machine and I taught him a little about how it worked. It was a gear-hobbing machine that made gears for transmissions and the like. We had several already, but this one had some capabilities that the others didn't. So that day he learned a little about gears, and how they were made.

For the rest of the week and on into the next week as well, Jess buried himself in work around the shop. He seemed to be out of his depressed mood after our trip to Bay City, so I saw no need in bringing it up. But it was unusual for a boy his age to be working as hard as he was during his summer vacation.

Meanwhile, Jess's friends and little brother were seeing very little of him. He was always at my shop before me on the Orange Krate. So he was always gone before Brian got up.

"What's the deal, man? How's your brother?," John David asked Brian, during lunch at Fred's. "Is he still messed up about the race, or what?"

"I don't know. I hardly ever see him. He's at work with dad early. And when he comes home, he usually goes right to bed. He gets mad if I try to talk to him. So I just stay out of his way," Brian told him.

"Not that I blame him for not coming around," Shawn said. "That Zack has been one big pain in the butt ever since the wreck."

They were looking at the booth, which used to belong to Jess and the Go-Kart Alley boys, now occupied by Zack and his gang.

"He just brags and brags. I don't think a day has gone by that he hasn't reminded me that he won the race, *before* Jess wrecked. I wish he'd shut up," Shawn said.

"I wish Jess hadn't given up so easy. He was the best. He could have found a way to beat Zack. We all would have helped," John David said.

"But that's not the way Jess wanted it. He wanted to do it himself. Still it is kind of hard to believe he just gave up like that," Brian said.

"I wish he'd at least go see Josie. Or call or write, or something! I can't stand her pestering me about him every time I try to mow the lawn up there," John David said.

"Look at that punk!" Shawn said, looking at Zack who was showing off to his buddies. "Somebody needs to take him down."

Chapter 17

Another week and a half went by until Brian was awakened rudely in his early morning slumber.

"What! What is it?," Brian grumbled, trying to hide the light from hitting his squinted eyes.

"Shhh! Come on, get dressed. I've got to show you something."

Brian stumbled from his bed and made his way to some clothes. Rubbing his eyes, he followed his brother. Through the dark, they made their way out to the shed. Jess rolled up the door and turned on one light.

Brian's mouth fell open as he finally stopped rubbing sleep from his eyes. There in the glow of a single light bulb shining brilliantly, was a miniature mock-up of a '32 Ford deuce coupe, painted shiny black with red, orange and yellow flames down the side. There was chrome and polished aluminum everywhere it could be except for the grill. It was painted cherry red. It was Jess's new go-kart!

"Wh…Where did you get it?," Brian asked in awe.

"I made it. Don't I make everything?," Jess said sarcastically to his brother.

"But how did you afford the parts for something like this," Brian said, getting a closer look at the kart. "It must have cost a fortune."

"From a junkpile, of course. Only, a new junkpile I found access to," Jess told him. "See, I been learning the ins and outs of Dad's shop these past three weeks. There's a lot of good stuff that goes into the scrap bin down there."

"But these are all good parts. Or else they wouldn't work, right?"

"Good for me, yeah. But they were all scrapped for other reasons that made them not work for what they were made for."

"I'm confused," Brian said, sitting. "What was dad doing making go-kart parts?"

"He wasn't. These were all for something else. I just made

'em work for a go-kart," Jess said. "Let me explain. See, I had almost given up on go-karting until one day when I was checking in castings for some air compressor blocks we were supposed to run. My job was to check to make sure there were no defects in them that we couldn't fix. If there were, I had to send them back to the casting company. I found two that had problems which made them scrap, but I couldn't send them back. They had given me an idea. I didn't know what exactly I would use them for, but I hid them off to the side, just in case. Then I fudged on the paperwork, so that no one would miss them.

"They kept working on my mind, until I started thinking about go-karts again. And when I did, I started thinking of ways to beat Zack. The more I thought, the madder I got, and the harder I thought of ways to beat him.

"I was trying to understand how he beat me. I didn't know how those little chainsaw engines could be so fast. On a trip to Bay City with dad in 'Old Red' I figured it out. He was telling me about two-cycle engines, and it got me to thinking about Zack's two chainsaw engines, which are two-cycle.

"The way they work, one two-cycle cylinder provides the power of two four-cycle cylinders, because it fires every time it comes to the top. So, with two ten-horsepower two-cycle engines, it's like he has a twenty-horsepower, four-cylinder, four-cycle engine. I just had to think of a way to beat that and still be original. I didn't want to copycat him by just using chainsaw engines. So I dreamt up this."

Jess went over his new go-kart in great detail with Brian. He was explaining why he had made the engine in the front, between the driver's legs, rather than in the back like a traditional go-kart.

"I wanted to be original, and I had never seen a go-kart with the motor in the front like a car, so I decided that is what I wanted to do. This small engine up front is an in-line, two-cylinder, supercharged power plant. I made it by bolting two modified air compressor blocks together. The crankshaft is made from a very small four-cylinder tractor engine's crankshaft, cut in half.

"On top of the blocks are two blowers, one for each cylinder, that I salvaged from scrap. They were actually intended to be small twin-screw, inert gas compressors for a petrochemical plant, but the screws inside were ground too far undersized to be any good. Their housings were milled too oversized as well. So, combining the two defects made them perfect for what I wanted. If the screws didn't fit so loosely in the housing, the blowers would be so powerful they would literally blow the engine apart," Jess said.

"How do they work, and what is a screw?," Brian asked.

"There are two screws inside that are like two spiral gears rolling together. The way they roll together draws air into one side, and pushes it out the discharge side.

"The discharge side is right over the top of the piston. I mounted two downdraft carburetors that I ordered from Carl, one on each blower. Each one has its own air cleaner, both encased in this nifty, polished aluminum hood scoop I made to look like the race cars.

"I used the 'feed engage' clutch off some old machinery dad was getting rid of for my drive clutch. It's here at the back of the engine. There wasn't enough room to put the whole transmission here, so I put gears one and two up front. A drive shaft runs just under the seat. And gears three and reverse are in the back."

"Whoa! Reverse?," Brian asked.

"Yep. Three speed with reverse," Jess said. "The frame and body are all aluminum. The body is reinforced with steel tubing, and the roll bars are made from chrome-molybdenum tubing. I wanted them to be strong, because the roll bars on the Heatseeker probably saved my life."

"Dad let you build all this during day shift?," said Brian.

"I don't know if you would say 'let me'. I kinda did it without asking. As a matter of fact, it was a pretty complicated ordeal how I managed to get it built, and so quickly.

"Once I figured out how I wanted it to look, I started designing the frame and body around the two compressor blocks. I set them together between my legs and got my measurements down. Then I went to the computer whenever I had spare time. I used the CAD program to draw up my go-kart plans.

"I had to save the drawings under names that dad wouldn't think to look at. Most of my parts were going to be made out of parts we already ran at the shop. I just needed to modify them to work for my go-kart. So I copied existing drawings and made my modifications to them. Then I gave them the same part number but added a new suffix that would only be for my parts. Like the 426-440-383-003 part number for the compressor blocks, I changed to 426-440-383-005.

"I could have never been able to set up the machines to run my parts and make it work. So I studied where each job was running and when they were going to run out of work. If there was going to be a set up on second shift right away, I laid out my parts and blueprints to be setup next. Labeling them as 'hot jobs'.

"At the first of the shift, they would set up and run my one or two parts, and then make another set up for regular work."

"But wouldn't that have set second shift behind on production? Dad watches that pretty closely. If they didn't run enough parts, he would want to know why," Brian said.

"That's where I came in. By the time second shift was back running regular production parts, it was time to lock up and go home. Just after they left, I unlocked the doors, turned on the machines, and started running production. While the machines ran, I was busy changing paperwork so that second shift production looked good, and dad would be none the wiser.

"It wasn't easy staging the work for second shift, especially without dad finding out. I had to really be on top of things on day shift to get everything ready. I pulled it off by working hard and letting dad know he could trust me to do many different jobs around the shop. Which he could, but I just added a little extra effort to even out my double-dealings.

"I also had a hard time keeping it from you. I was exhausted when I got home from first shift, and I needed to get some sleep before starting the graveyard shift. I wanted to hang out with you and tell you all about it when I got home, but I knew I needed to get some sleep. At one eleven o'clock every night, I got up and went out to the barn where I was hiding all my parts. I loaded what I needed onto the truck and pushed it down the hill behind our shop before starting it, so I wouldn't wake anybody. I went to dad's shop and hung out outside, waiting for all the workers to leave. Then I snuck in and when to work.

"It was hard not to let time get away from me. I had to keep a close eye on the clock so I would have time to clean up whatever I was working on, load it up, and carry it back to the barn. I had to put the truck back just like I found it and ride the Orange Krate back to dad's shop. Then I would act like I got there early and started warming up the machines. That way no one would be able to tell that they had been running all night.

"One day things just started to click, and it didn't take long to run all of the parts I needed to build my go-kart. I had the gear department making my gears disguised as tractor gears. The sheet metal department made the body one piece at a time which, they thought, were pieces of ductwork for a large building in Prichard. The engine blocks ran on the mills as new experimental air compressors. Various other pieces and parts were given vague names to describe their apparent use, like clevis or hinge pin.

"It was a nightmare covering my paper trail, but I was able to do it. The last few nights I spent painting and assembling it here at our shop. I've had the engine running, and the transmission powered up by an electric motor at dad's, but I haven't driven it yet. I need your help to get it down to the trail and test it out. I need to work out all of the bugs and see if all my efforts are gonna pay off in beating Zack."

Brian helped Jess load the kart on the truck and push it down the hill. Jess popped the clutch on the truck and used the momentum from the hill to start the engine. Brian hopped on and they rode down to the trail by the light of the lone headlamp on the truck.

At the trail they rolled the super coupe down plank ramps,

off the truck and onto the trail. Jess crawled in and sat for a moment admiring the stillness of the early morning, listening to the chirp of cricket songs in the calm darkness. Then he pushed the starter button. Varoooom! went the supercharged two-cycle engine. It would have definitely been too loud to start near the house at that time in the morning. But down on the trail outside of town, there was no one to wake except cows and a few raccoons.

Jess revved the engine a little and then let it idle for a while to get warmed up. Jess had separated his legs from the hot engines with a sheet metal barrier covered in some leftover fire blanket used to insulated the heat-treat ovens at my shop. It held back most of the heat fairly well.

Satisfied that the new engine was warmed up and running smoothly, Jess turned on the small side lights, put it in gear and slowly let out the clutch. He made very slow and smooth transitions between gears, making sure everything worked properly. He kept this up, back and forth on the trail, until he felt everything was working alright. Then he started speeding it up a bit. Then a little more, until finally he was ready to start checking his time in the eighth-mile.

Jess got at one end of the dragstrip, and Brian was at the other. When Jess flashed his lights, Brian started the stopwatch as Jess took off. Then Brian would check the time, as Jess came barreling past. His time started off kind of slow, but constantly got faster and faster, until it finally leveled off.

"Well, your time is pretty consistent," Brian told Jess as he pulled up and stopped. "Have you got it as fast as it will go?"

"Brian," Jess said, "I've got it as fast as I want to go. I never thought I would reach a speed that I thought was too fast on a go-kart, but I've done it tonight. I don't know just how fast this will go, but I know if it ever reaches top speed, it better have wings on it."

It was beginning to show a little daylight in the east, so they carried the go-kart back to the barn and hid it where Go-Kart Alley customers wouldn't see it. When they put the truck back in the shop, Jess started telling Brian about a plan he had been hatching ever since he had started building the little deuce coupe.

"I not only want to beat Zack, I want to put a little fear in him. I've seen him around showing off to his buddies and everyone else who will pay attention to him. I want him to look like a goof, so they'll all know how fake he is," Jess told him.

"What do you plan to do?," Brian asked

"Here's how it'll start…"

Jess revealed his plan in detail to Brian as they closed up the shop and headed back to the house.

Chapter 18

Jess played sick that day to get out of going to the shop with me, now that he was finished with his kart and all. Plus, he just wanted to get some rest before carrying out his plan.

Late that night Brian helped Jess get the go-kart down to the trail once more. Jess had found an old helmet at the dump and painted it black. He put in on and started the deuce. Then he roared off towards town in the darkness.

He went through town and on out west towards Shady Grove. Out on a lonely stretch he came upon Zack's house, which backed up to the trail. From a high speed, Jess killed the motor and coasted silently off the trail and onto a loose gravel patch behind Zack's chain-link fenced backyard.

Coming to a quiet stop, he waited for everything to be calm. Then he whistled a faint, high-pitched whistle to get the dog's attention inside the fence.

When the dog heard the noise, he got up and came to the fence. When he noticed the black go-kart sitting out of place behind the fence, he began barking wildly. After a few minutes of barking, there came a voice from inside the house.

"Zackary!," Zack's mother called from one part of the house. "Go see what your dog is barking at!"

There was a delay, and then the window finally came open.

"Hey! Shut up, you stupid...," Zack began to call out the window before freezing in his tracks at the sight of the deuce under the yard light.

Jess fired up the kart and then revved the engine loudly. He popped the clutch and spun out directly towards the fence before cutting the wheels and making a 180-degree turn towards the trail. In a cloud of dust followed by squealing tires, he was gone.

Zack stared in shock at the settling dust under the yard light. Still half asleep, he wondered, "Was it real," or had he dreamed it? He had an uneasy feeling getting back to sleep, unable to get the ghostly image of the black phantom go-kart out of his mind.

Meanwhile the "phantom" was blowing through Sumner at a high rate of speed, flying down the deserted trail. The loud roar of the engine echoed through the sleepy small town, drawing attention from every dog in every yard.

Jess housed the kart back in the barn and let Brian in on "stage two" of his plan.

That morning, Jess had cut a deal with the owner of the property next to Fred's to cut down an old tree that overhung Fred's fence. Then he paid a man who cut firewood to do the job for him. He paid a little extra for him to follow specific instructions. Not only was he to cut down the tree, but also he had to start at precisely 12:40 that afternoon. The man agreed and set his watch with Jess's.

At eleven-thirty, Brian met the guys up at Fred's for lunch as usual. Jess went back to work at my shop for a day to make his schedule look normal. Occasionally, during his three-week return to my shop, Jess could be seen driving the Orange Krate home for lunch at quarter after noon, and back again at quarter to one. This day would be no different.

Zack's buddies gathered early at Jess's old booth before Zack arrived. When he showed up, he was later than normal and a little excited.

"Hey!," he said to his companions, in a hushed tone. "Have you guys seen a black go-kart around today?"

"Well, there's one over there, and one over there, and I think yours is black," one guy said sarcastically.

"Smart-aleck! No, I mean one you haven't seen before. It's black with flames down it, and it looks like…like one of those old-timey cars," Zack explained. "And it looks pretty fast."

"Why, is someone looking to race you?," the guy asked.

"I dunno, maybe," Zack said.

"Well, are they or not. When did you see it?"

"I don't know if I saw it. The dog woke me up last night, and when I looked outside it was there, but then it was gone," Zack told them. "Has anyone seen McCormick today?"

"Why, you getting nervous on top there, buddy? Can't handle the pressure of being the fastest? Seeing ghost-karts in the middle of the night?" His friend laughed, followed by the laughter of all at the table.

"Shut up!," Zack told them.

"Yeah, we seen him goin' home on his old orange kart just before you got here," one said.

Brian struggled to hear what they were talking about. He couldn't make out everything. But he figured by the way Zack was acting and the reaction of his buddies, that Jess's plan was working.

Things calmed down, and Zack began to dismiss his fears about what he had seen. It wasn't long before he was back acting up and showing off to his buddies. He had to show them who was boss again after they had taunted him. He even got up and made some pot shots at Brian about Jess.

Brian had taken constant ribbing from Zack ever since Jess's wreck. But this day he secretly grinned inside during the abuse, knowing what was in store for Zack. Brian usually ignored him and did just the same this day.

He sat there with Shawn and John David and enjoyed his lunch, with a keen eye on his watch. By twelve-thirty he began to feel a little excited but tried not to show it. By twelve thirty-five the anticipation was almost unbearable. Another two minutes ticked by, and Brian saw the man carry his chainsaw out to where the old dead tree hung over the fence. The man stood there a while looking at his watch.

When Jess had come by Fred's on the Orange Krate, he wasn't headed to the house. He was going to Harvey's junkyard. When he got there, he greeted Harvey. Sloppy didn't get up to meet him.

"She's in da shed purty as ya left 'er," Harvey told him. "Dat was a good piece of werk ya did dar'."

"Thanks. I just hope I did enough," Jess told him.

Jess visited with the old German for a while. At 11:35 he parked the Orange Krate around back of Harvey's shed and went in the back door. Inside sat the deuce, shined up and ready to go. Jess pushed it outside and got in. He put on the black helmet and started the engine. He looked at his watch. It was twelve thirty-seven. Jess waved 'bye to Harvey and took off to the trail.

"Give 'er!" Harvey called to him, as he sped off.

Jess turned right on the trail and went out a little outside of town to get some starting distance. Then he whipped around and headed back into town. Carefully watching the time, he cruised at a moderate speed. When he got a little further into town and it turned twelve thirty-nine, Jess punched it up to high speed.

At twelve thirty-nine and fifty-five seconds, Jess let off the gas and pushed in the clutch to coast quietly. At exactly twelve thirty-nine and fifty-nine seconds, Jess hit the gas with a loud roar right as he passed Fred's first fence. Zack's head swiveled around in an instant at the eerie sound he had heard before. Just as he did, he caught sight of the phantom go-kart once again. In a flash, it was out of sight. At exactly twelve forty, the man started his large chainsaw and revved it up loudly, as Jess had asked.

Zack only let out an excited grunt and pointed to the trail. His friends turned to see what he was looking at.

"Did you see it?," Zack said

"See what?," one friend asked.

"The go-kart! It was here. It just went past. Didn't you hear it? It was loud, like a big chainsaw, but different! You had to hear it!," Zack said, almost yelling with excitement.

"Like that chainsaw over there? Man, you're losing it" the friend dismissed Zack's concern.

Zack got up and went directly over to Brian and grabbed him by the shirt.

"Where's your brother, huh? Where is he? Did he get a new kart? What's the deal, huh? What are you trying to pull? Huh? Answer me!," Zack said, screaming.

John David got up and quickly intervened. The stout football player bear hugged Zack from behind, causing him to let go of Brian. Then with tackling force he pushed Zack out away from the table.

"You better calm down. Nobody knows what the heck you're talking about. So, why don't you just go sit down at your little 'cool table' and chill out," John David told him.

Jess went at full speed towards the highway by the shop

and didn't slow down until he got there. Downshifting and using the brakes, he brought down his speed and exited the trail just before the bridge over the highway. He pulled onto the shoulder of the highway and went north one quarter of a mile at high speed again to a small paved road that paralleled the trail. He slowed for the turn onto the road, and then gunned his speed back up.

If he had seen a cop, he would have gotten a ticket for speeding, as well as using a go-kart on the public roads. Heading in the direction of Harvey's, he made it down the road where he actually passed two cars. Downshifting again, he made a quick right turn onto a small path that led to the trail and came out right across from the junkyard.

He crossed the trail and pulled into Harvey's, parked the deuce in the shed and got back on the Orange Krate and headed back to my shop. He was going past Fred's at 11:45, his usual time, and moving in the same direction that the phantom had gone and not come back from.

"There goes Jess now, you goof! Man, picking on that little kid because you're scared. You're really losing it," one buddy told Zack.

"Shut up. I know what I saw!," he returned.

That afternoon when Jess got home, he couldn't wait to hear how his plan worked. Brian told him all about it and how Zack started freaking out.

"You should have seen it. He even grabbed me and started shaking me, wanting to know where you were. It was perfect. You've really got him paranoid now," Brian told him, laughing and acting out Zack's excitement. "Where is he? Huh? Huh?"

"Well, it won't be long now. I'll wait until I know everyone is there, just like he did me. I just hope he hasn't made my booth too gross to sit at anymore," Jess said.

The two brothers went over to the truck to untarp and unload the deuce. Brian had gone down to Harvey's with the truck during the afternoon, and he had hauled back the deuce. He covered it with a tarp and added some extra pieces underneath so as to not give away its shape. When the sun began to dim and the air hinted at cooling off, they knew Fred's would soon be packed and Zack would be back acting up for attention.

Brian got ready to leave at his regular time. Just before he did, he spoke to Jess.

"Are you ready? You look a little nervous."

"Well, that last race was kinda hairy. I'm just trying to get myself psyched up. That's all," Jess told him.

"It'll be alright, man. You're the best. It's time to remind everyone."

"Thanks, man. I couldn't have done it without you. Half that motor was your idea. The two cylinders, the crankshaft, ignition, and carburetors were all yours. Did you think no one was reading all of those napkins you brought home from Fred's with notes written on them?," Jess said with a grin.

"I thought a lot of that looked familiar, you sorry thief!," Brian said.

"Well, you better get going," Jess told him.

With that, Brian took of down the path on his antique Yazoo Dragster. Jess paced around the shop for a while, sat down, but stood back up again. He stepped outside and listened for go-karts moving down the trail towards Fred's.

Walking around the building, he came to the old ratty tarp covering a lumpy mass. He pulled up one corner to look at the twisted wreckage of the Heatseeker underneath.

"Well, you were a good go-kart. I learned a lot from you. Now it's time to show everyone how much," Jess told it.

Figuring it was about time, Jess got in his kart and put on the helmet. The engine roared to life, then idled until it was warmed up. With squealing tires and blue smoke, the deuce screamed out of the shed, spun through the gravel, and flew down the backpath.

Everyone was at Fred's, and the place was packed. It was Friday night, Engine Joe was playing, and the house was rockin'. Zack was there and sitting with his gang in the booth by the window. Music was playing loud and friends struggled to talk to one another over the noise. Fred was busy carrying hot, delicious pizzas out to the hungry kids, and empty pans back to the kitchen. It was probably the busiest night the little restaurant had seen all summer.

Jess slid all sideways as he came off the backpath and onto the trail in his high-powered new go-kart. He floored it and headed towards the busy restaurant. Every nerve in his body was tingling with anticipation of what was going to go down. It had been a while since he had raced, and he was longing to do it again. Only this time he hoped the results would be better.

When he made it into town, he barely slowed down to make the turn into Fred's. His engine growled loudly from a quick downshift and heavy brakes as he made the turn. He was headed straight for the swinging glass door into the backroom.

The noise could not be heard at first over the sound of the gathering inside. It wasn't until the black go-kart came to a stop, only inches from the door, and revved its powerful engine, that everyone took notice.

A hush fell over the gang inside. The band stopped playing, kids stopped talking, quarters went to waste in video games, and Zack stopped showing off. The only sound, other than the gentle idle of the black go-kart's motor, was Fred and his staff toiling away in the kitchen.

Zack knew the sound and what was going on. He slowly turned his head to look towards the door. The phantom go-kart he was seeing was suddenly very real to him. He swallowed a drink of Sun-drop.

The Phantom Driver raised a hand in a black glove and pointed to Zack, and then nodded as if to say, "That's right. I want you!"

Zack started to stand up from the booth while his buddies egged him on. As he did, The Phantom Driver put the black deuce into reverse and squealed quickly back from the door and slung around 90 degrees. There was another hush over the crowd at the sight of a go-kart with reverse. Then the black go-kart lunged forward, leaving out for the drag strip in a cloud of blue smoke.

Zack and his buddies followed next, and then Brian,

Shawn, John David, Roman and everyone else from inside. There was something cool and mysterious about Zack's new challenger, and everyone wanted to find out who he was.

Jess waited nervously at the start line. He figured that he had taken Zack by surprise and didn't anticipate any mysterious boulders rolling down the hill. He finally saw Zack coming up, along with the rest of the crowd. Brian got there fast and quickly jumped out to flag the race.

When everyone was around to watch, Brian started the countdown. Zack was acting jerky and restless, trying to be tough and acting like he was checking out his kart. He wanted to look like he knew what he was doing. He wanted to look like he wasn't scared.

"Come on! Let's do this!," he shouted in false eagerness.

"On your mark...Get set..." Brian counted.

Jess turned his helmet to see Zack still jerking around like he was getting ready to ride a bull. Then he turned back to the trail, now with full confidence.

"GO!" Brian shouted.

The deuce squealed tires and left black marks for fifteen feet. Then grabbed second gear, followed by some more squealing. Even with the loss of traction, the deuce had pulled farther off the line than Zack's demon kart. It continued to move away in second gear. Third gear carried the kart all the way to the end by the time Zack was halfway down.

Jess made his way off the trail onto the loose gravel, slid sideways for twenty feet, and turned around 180 degrees. He dropped it to second, and kept it floored. His go-kart was actually sliding backwards to a stop as his tires spun forward in the gravel. He made it back onto the trail before Zack had reached the end of the strip.

Jess unfastened his helmet with one hand and took it off. As he passed Zack, he gave it a toss and let it fly up over Zack and roll down the steep embankment on the other side.

Jess barely gave a glance to Zack as he sped past headed back to Fred's. He never slowed down past all the spectators. He just flew through a gap in the road and sped back to reclaim his booth at the pizza place. All of the crowd jumped on their go-karts and followed suit. All except Zack. He went home, and didn't return to Fred's for the rest of the summer.

Chapter 19

Fred had the booth cleaned and ready for Jess when he returned. He was sitting and waiting for a thick-crust, double pepperoni and ice-cold Sun-drop when the rest of the crowd returned.

There was quite a buzz when they got there. Everyone wanted to know about the go-kart and what kind of motor it had, to beat Zack the way it did. Jess went out and proudly showed off his handiwork. The bandleader shook Jess' hand in congratulations before returning to the stage to play an almost terrible, but still cool, unrehearsed rendition of Little Deuce Coupe.

Jess came back inside to eat his pizza, and Brian, John David and Shawn all followed, talking his ear off--all glad to see him back where he belonged.

They were laughing and visiting, and everything was back to normal. Jess shared the story about how he was able to build the deuce and how he and Brian carried out his plan. The others filled Jess in on what all had gone on around there while he was away.

Jess was listening intently and enjoying his pizza, when he suddenly dropped his slice and blocked out all that was being said to him. He got up and made a beeline for the bulletin board.

Shawn was in the middle of a story when he realized Jess wasn't listening and tapered off in midsentence. All three were looking at Jess to see where he was going.

A newspaper article was posted on the board that caught Jess's eye. The article from the previous week's paper was newly posted on the board. It had a headline which read, "Junior Drag Racing League Runs With The Big Boys," and was accompanied by a picture.

Jess glanced through the article and looked at the picture. He caught Fred as he walked by.

"Hey, Fred. Did you put this up here?," Jess asked him.

"Yeah, I was reading about that yesterday. I thought you kids might be interested in it," he said.

"Thanks."

Jess pulled out the thumbtacks and took the article over to show the others.

"Check this out, guys. There's a program that lets kids drag race at Bay City Speedway," he told them.

"Race in what?," Shawn asked.

"In Jr. Dragsters. It says here that this is their third year in Bay City. It started when a guy built a half-scale drag car for his kids, powered by a go-kart engine. A few more followed, and they began having competition in the off time of the track. Several others tracks picked up on it in the past two years, and they just moved races up to Friday nights along with big car races in order to gain more spectators. This year they plan to have a season-ending finals race between the toughest competitors from area drag strips."

"Cool!"

"Jr. Drag racing is open to ages eight through fifteen in two classes, Sportsman and Modified. Ages twelve through fifteen are in Modified class and are allowed to run faster cars. It gives the kids a chance to practice real bracket racing, like with the big cars.

"The reporter questions the safety issue, and the guy states that it is totally safe. They've only had one accident since the trend began, and it was a girl who rolled her car on her first-ever run. It seems her dad told her to go as fast as she could, but neglected to tell her to slow down when she turned off the track. The car proved to be safe. She walked away uninjured. The parents were more shaken up than she was."

"Does it say how you can get into it?," Brian asked.

"It says to call the track in Bay City for information on the sport."

It was Friday evening, the time the races were going on, so Jess decided to call the track to find out more about the sport. It sounded hectic at the track, and he had to speak to several people and wait a long time before he got to talk to the director of the Jr. program.

Jess explained who he was and where he found out about them.

"Yes, it seems we've been getting a lot of calls since the article came out. The best way to find out about the program is by reading the rulebook. All of the area tracks are following standard rules this year, so we can participate in the season finals together. You say you are in Sumner? We have a couple of racers from Sand Flat. I could put you in touch with one of them, maybe send a rulebook and some entry forms home with one guy tonight.

"We also have a Jr. Dragster racing school on Wednesday nights you can attend to get familiar with how it works. There's a track car there to drive, or you can bring your own.

"I'll tell you what. We're kinda busy right now. Let me get in touch with one guy and call you back. Do you have a number I can reach you at?"

Jess gave him the number to the Fred's payphone along with his home number. The guys pored over the article while they waited for a return phone call.

"Man," Shawn said, "we need to get into this. With our combined go-kart talents, we could be the coolest crew there. I bet you can win prizes and stuff, too."

The wheels in their heads began turning, and they began to think up different motors to put on their car. They even contemplated trying to get another motor like the Deuce's built, but they knew that would be impossible to do again.

Finally, the man called back. He told Jess that someone would meet them in Sand Flat at Frosty's around noon with the information.

The guys continued to dream about the Go-Kart Alley Jr. dragster. When it got late, they headed to the go-kart shop to draw out some designs on graph paper. The whole idea of real drag racing had them all excited. They stayed up late and camped out in the shop, catching up with Jess, listening to the radio and making dragster plans.

The next day, they headed over to Frosty's to get their rulebook. When they got there, they didn't find anyone who looked like they were there with the information. Jess asked Josie's uncle if she would be working that day.

"Not today. They stopped in earlier on their way up north. She and her dad left this for you, said you'd be here looking for it," her uncle told him.

He handed Jess a small paper book and several forms. Jess took them and looked them over. It was the Jr. Drag Racing League rulebook and entry forms. He then looked puzzled at him.

"Why did she have it?," Jess asked.

"They said you called the race track last night and wanted to get into it."

"They were the ones from Sand Flat that were there?"

"Yeah. Josie races the Frosty's car. You didn't know that? She's just started this year in the Sportsman class. Rolled her car on her first run, ha ha. Wasn't hurt, though. Last night was her first night back. Did pretty good, too." He pointed to a picture on the wall of Josie and her car. "She wouldn't let me put that up until she got going again."

"She never said anything to me about it. Last night was the first I've ever even heard about Jr. drag racing."

"Well, that book ought to fill you in some. Her dad can tell you all about it when he gets back. They went out of town for a few days to visit some family."

They took the information, thanked her uncle, and headed back to the shop. When they got there, the guys had to pick on Jess about his girlfriend being in drag racing before him.

"Man, I feel like an idiot, the way I explained all my go-kart stuff to her, like she didn't know anything about it. She probably knows more about it than me!," Jess said.

They read through the rulebook several times trying to get the gist of everything. Some of it was hard for them to understand because it used terms they were not familiar with like; red light, breakout, dial-in and elapsed time. They didn't pay too much attention to it, for they figured they could pick all that up at the school on Wednesday.

What they did pay attention to were the rules concerning the frame, engine, brakes and safety equipment; especially the engine rules. It stated that:

All vehicles restricted to a maximum of one, rear-mounted,

5-HP four-cycle Briggs & Stratton engine. Must retain Briggs & Stratton 5-HP engine block in unaltered "as cast" condition. Porting, polishing, and relieving of block, machining of deck surface permitted. Aftermarket head permitted.

It went on to prohibit all superchargers and turbochargers. The rules pretty much shot down all of the plans the boys had made as far as an engine. The only bonus they saw, was that the burning of alcohol was permitted.

"Man! What fun is it if all you get to run is a five-horse." Jess said.

"Hey!," Brian said. "Some of us happen to like the five-horse Briggs."

Getting past the motor restrictions, they learned of the time restriction on the different classes. Sportsman class, which Josie was in because she didn't turn twelve until September, could not run a 1/8-mile in less than 12.90 seconds. Modified, which the boys would be in, could not run faster than 7.90 seconds.

When they were done complaining about the restrictions, they began concentrating on the frame and body. The book had detailed information on how the frame had to be constructed for safety reasons. It also had drawings with wheelbase sizes and tube diameter sizes for different kinds of metals.

Other things it covered concerning the frame, were roll cages and driver compartment, deflector plates, steering, foot box and bulkhead. It was very thorough, and the boys had plenty of knowledge to begin rustling up parts to build it out of.

They made a note of what they had at the shop and then headed to Harvey's to look around some more. Brian knew of a good 5-HP block down there, that he had stashed off to the side.

They got there and visited with Harvey under the awning like they always did. It was part of their payment for getting to use the junkyard. They didn't mind. He always had an interesting story to tell.

Everyone pulled up a lawn chair or wooden box and sat

down. Brian was the first to notice someone was missing.

"Where's Sloppy? The heat get to him, and he didn't want to come out from under the house?," he asked.

"I wish it was jus da heat. He's at da vet. Doc says he got 'hip displacea.' Fancy talk for cost a lot of money," Harvey told them. "He says he gotta have a big surgery."

"Is that where he is, getting the surgery done?," Brian asked.

"No, the vet, he just wanted to watch him for a while. I can't afford no surgery for him now. Vet says I can't put it off much longer, else he'll be in too much pain, and I'll have to put him down."

"Not Sloppy!," Jess said. "He's been around as long as I can remember. What are you gonna do?"

"Well, it cost about tree tousand. I could probably get that much if I sold off the junkyard for scrap metal. The city has been after me to clean up my junk for a while, not to mention all these fancy folks walking up this trail. I tell them it's an antique décor, but they call it junk"

The boys were horrified at the thought of losing their junk supply, almost as much as they were about Sloppy being put to sleep. It was as if their happy little go-kart world were crumbling around them.

"Well, you boys go on and get what you need before it's gone. I'm gonna go inside where it's cool," Harvey said, before getting up to walk inside.

Bummed, the boys made their rounds in the junkyard and picked out a few things they might need. They gathered them up and loaded them on the truck. Jess left a few bucks in his mailbox to cover the cost.

They picked up some steel tubing from my shop and returned to the go-kart shop, where they began laying out the frame. Brian stripped down the motor and cleaned up the block. He began puzzling over how to get more power out of the little engine, thinking of all of the tricks that Harvey had told him about.

Chapter 20

By Wednesday morning they had a rough half-scale dragster frame tacked together, spanning the worktables in their shop. There was no suspension or motor mounts yet, for they hadn't been able to find any tires or wheels like the ones on the other dragsters in the pictures of the rulebook. They had to put off a lot of their work until they got a chance to look at one up close and find out where to get parts.

Jess tried calling Josie all that week, so he could get a hold of her as soon as she got back. He wanted to apologize for not contacting her over the past three weeks since the Heatseeker wreck. He also wanted to ask her about Jr. drag racing. There was finally an answer at her house Wednesday afternoon. He was nervous when he heard her voice on the other end, hoping she wouldn't be mad at him.

"Jess!," she exclaimed. "I thought you'd fallen off the face of the earth!"

"Sorry about not calling or coming by to see you. I had a kind of rough time these past few weeks."

"I know. I saw John David at his grandmother's, and he told me about your accident. I was sorry to hear about your go-kart, but I was glad you were OK."

"I hear you had a little spill as well," Jess said, trying to coax her secret out of her.

"Oh, you heard, huh? Yeah, I was kind of embarrassed about that, but I guess you can relate."

"How come you never told me about Jr. drag racing?"

"Well, I didn't meet you until after I had my accident. I wasn't sure if I would race again, so I just didn't want to say anything."

Jess could understand that. He told her about his new go-kart and how he managed to get the revolutionary engine built at my shop, and why he had been too busy to call. She was not mad, although she did get her feelings hurt a little when he stopped calling on her. She shared some news with him that brought him down when he heard it.

Dennis R. Van Vleet

When Jess never called, she started talking to Tony again. She said he was being very sweet at first, but it wasn't long before he started being a jerk again. She found out that he was Zack's cousin, and they had plotted together to beat Jess. Tony's older brothers, who build race cars, turned Zack's old go-kart into the demon kart. He said they stole the chainsaw engines from a logging company that was clearing land next to theirs.

Jess's heart sank when he was stabbed and shot with the thought of someone else talking to Josie. But she went on to tell him more. Tony also told her that he was the one who rolled the rock down the hill that caused the Heatseeker to crash.

"He was supposed to do it only if you were winning, but he did it anyway. He said it slipped, but I know he did it on purpose," She said.

"Why, that snake! I'm gonna beat his...," Jess began angrily.

"No! You can't. He would know I told you," she pleaded.

She heard how Jess was getting upset and didn't have the heart to tell him what else she knew about Tony.

"Besides he's just a jerk, a loser. You should just be the bigger man and know that you are better than him. I don't care if I never talk to him again," she said.

"Well, maybe you're right. Anyway, I've got a new go-kart now, and no one can beat it. I've got a successful go-kart shop, and we're gonna have our own Jr. dragster. Let's see Tony top that."

They talked about the racing school, and she told him she would be there. Her dad was the instructor, and she was coming to get some practice time in at the track. She said her car would be there, along with a few others so they would get a chance to see how they were built and get some ideas for their own. Her dad was the best small-engine builder at the track, and she would talk him into giving Brian a few pointers.

Jess got off the phone feeling better but still bothered by Tony. He told the others about it, and they got mad as well. John David threatened to drive to Sand Flat and put some of his football skill to work on Tony, but Jess talked him down and shared Josie's advice.

They set their minds to building the best Jr. dragster they could and focused their energy on being the bigger men. They left early to get to the track in time to do some looking around before the class started.

It was a long drive to the speedway in Bay City, about twenty miles. The dragstrip sat just this side of the big town, in the country, and right off the old railroad right-of-way. Most of the drive was forbidden for the hardship rule only gave them passage thru Clearwater County. The track was a good fifteen miles into the Spearman County. Large signs expressly forbid the use of motor vehicles beyond Sand Flat. They carried plenty of fuel and kept an eye out for anyone who might turn them in.

They were in agreement that if they were spotted, they would duck off the trail, split up, and meet up at the track. Luckily, they managed to make the drive without being turned in. They got in and parked their karts under some trees behind the bleachers. Josie was already there, and she came out to greet them, commenting on Jess's new kart.

Jess showed her all of the things he had told her about over the phone, but, was more eager to hear about her car. The boys gave her car a good looking over, as well as the other cars there. They were very impressed. All of them were so professionally done, shiny and chrome, with professional paint jobs. They were long and slender, with fat tires on the back and tall skinny ones on the front, just like the dragsters you see on TV with the wing up in the back. But these lacked the wing. The sight of them made the work the boys had been doing all summer seem kind of inferior.

Her dad came over, and she introduced Jess to him.

"Daddy, this is Jess," she told him.

"Nice to meet you, Jess. I hear you're quite the go-kart builder," he said.

"We thought we were, until we saw these," Jess told him.

"Oh, it's not that hard; just a little work and a lot of spit and polish and, of course money. So you think you might be interested in Jr. drag racing?," he asked.

"Yep. We want to build one and paint it with the name of our go-kart shop on it. This is my little brother, Brian, and my friends, John David, Shawn, and Roman. Brian's my engine man, and Roman is our paint specialist. The other two are gophers," Jess told him with a laugh.

"Pleased to meet you. Well, I'll be glad to help you all I can. We better head over to the track and get this started."

They walked over to a car that was sitting near the starting line. Josie's dad called the rest around and began his presentation.

He shed a lot of light on what they had read in the rulebook; it was making more sense to them now. They learned that "Bracket Racing," the style used on the track, was much different than the "Heads up" drag racing they were used to. There were electronic devices to help line up the cars, and tell exactly when they started and when they had completed the eighth mile. There were also lights that flagged the drivers, instead of the old "on your mark, get set, go." The strangest thing to them was the fact that a slower car could still beat a fast car.

Winning in bracket racing is based on your dial-in and reaction time, and not just who crosses the finish line first. Mr. Mayfield explained to them the purpose of time trials and how they helped you set your dial-in.

In time trials you run your car just like a race. Both cars go at the same time, but it is not a race. The devices at the track record how long it takes to go, called reaction time, how long it takes to cover the eighth mile, called elapsed time or E.T., and your top speed in miles per hour.

The most important thing to be concerned with is your E.T. When racing begins, you have to set a time for your car to run, and not beat it or you will be disqualified. So, if you run the track several times and you know your car can do it in 9.321 seconds one time and 9.311 seconds the next time, you could set you dial-in at 9.290 seconds. That is telling the track men that you can run it in 9.290 seconds and not any faster, which you proved in the time trials. If you end up running under your dial—in less time--like 9.100 seconds, it's called a breakout and you lose.

The purpose of the dial-in, is so that cars of different speeds can be run together. A slower car is given a head start over a faster car, based on their dial-ins. If a 9.29 second dial-in car is put up against a 9.00 car, the 9.29 car gets a .29 second head start, and its green light will go first followed by the other's. The two cars should reach the finish line at the same time based on their dials.

The other thing you look at in time trials, is your reaction time. That is the time it takes you to go, once you have been flagged off. There is a pole in between the lanes that is equipped with lights, and it's called "the tree". There are three yellow lights for each lane, and they blink on and off, one after the other, followed by a green light. There is one-half second between the last yellow light and the green "go" light. You try to get the jump on the green, by starting to go before the green light actually comes on. The time it takes you to start moving, between the last yellow and the green, is your reaction time. A perfect reaction time is .500 seconds, one-half second; anything longer, like .927, will hurt you, and may cause you to lose. Anything shorter, like a .464, is a foul start called a red light, and you definitely lose. The red light comes on for your lane in the event of a foul start.

So, if both cars have a reaction time over .500 seconds with no red-lights, and neither go faster than their dial-in, then the winner is the one who crosses the finish line first. If one car red-lights, the other is automatically the winner. And if one car breaks out, and the other got a green light, the other car wins. If both cars breakout, the winner is the one who still comes closest to their dial.

Top speed is nice to know, but it doesn't come into play that much, except in the Modified class. Modified class has a time limit of no faster than 7.90 seconds, or 85 miles per hour.

The boys were confused and a little disappointed. First, they learned they could only run a 5-horse, now they heard that a slow car could beat them. There were many rules, and it cost money. They were beginning to wonder if maybe they should just stick to their old "heads up" style of racing on the trail. But then Mr. Mayfield was finished explaining from the book, and he fired up two cars.

When he did, the boys knew they were in the right place. They stared, and marveled at the sound of the little tricked-out motors. Any thought they had that these cars were all looks and no show were gone. The sound was amazing. Standing behind the cars as they "staged" at the starting line, Jess made the comment that the loud popping sounds of the two engines sounded similar to someone lighting the extra fuse on a brick of Black Cat firecrackers.

All of the rules had been hard to understand, but the boys followed as best as they could. It helped when cars actually began running. There were experienced kids there were demonstrating in their own cars. They were very good, but did things on purpose, like red-lighting and breaking out — to demonstrate the rules.

Mr. Mayfield also explained to them how staging worked. There were two electric eyes that made invisible beams across each lane. When a beam is broken by something in its path, a light comes on, on the tree. The first beam is the prestage light, and the second is the staged light. When both are on, the car is in position to start.

When both cars had both stage lights on, the yellow lights went down the tree followed by two greens. Right away, there were billboards lighted up at the other end of the track, posting their reaction times. When they reached the other end, it posted their E.T. and top speed. They did this twice, and then decided on a dial-in for each car. Then they made a run, as if they were really racing on Friday night. The first one was done right, both cars had green lights and neither broke out. The winner was the car that crossed the finish line first.

Then they made another round with one purposely red-lighting by taking off first. The next run, one car purposely set his dial too high and broke out. All of the examples the drivers made, proved Mr. Mayfield's lesson well. It also showed how quickly the track equipment calculated the winner in so many different situations. It was easy to follow, then. The winner was the one with the win light on his billboard; it was just tricky figuring out how he got it.

By the end of the class, the boys had made several runs in the track car themselves. Brian had to drive Josie's car, because he was under twelve. Josie's car was an unmodified car for Sportsman class. It was all stock as far as cylinder bore and crank stroke, but there were a few tricks she was allowed to have that were still legal. It went 50.34 mph over the track, in 12.294 seconds.

Jess and the others drove a modified car like the one they were building. It was fast, and the sensation of the acceleration off the starting line was unreal. It ran the eighth mile in 8.185 seconds, with a top speed of 79.95 mph. The boys were very impressed and couldn't wait to get back to work.

After the class, they got some one-on-one time with Josie's dad. He gave them a lot of information--some they didn't want to hear. He gave them good tips, but he let them in on some of the costs it took to compete. Engine modifications and frame specifications were going to cost a lot of money. This wasn't too bothersome to them, for they figured they could get that done through me. But when he started getting into fiberglass bodies, safety equipment, good clutches and gears, tires and fuel, it started adding up fast. Even working liberally, using as many of their junkyard skills as possible, it would cost them over two thousand to build. They left the track with the strange feeling of disappointment over excitement.

Chapter 21

The next morning they were all back in the shop trying to plan out their next move. They just had to find a way to get that dragster built and enter the racing. There were pens to paper figuring and refiguring costs, based on some catalogues for parts that Mr. Mayfield had given them.

"There's just got to be a way to come up with the two thousand," Brian said.

"Do you know how much money that is? We've worked out butts off in this shop all summer and we've only got about eleven hundred between us. Besides, don't you think if we could get it that easy, that we might help Harvey out with Sloppy?," Jess told him.

"I wish we could do both," Brian said.

Jess thought about it for a moment.

"Maybe we can. Did anyone read anything in that rulebook about the season ending finals race?," he asked.

John David picked it up and thumbed to the back. He found a small section that they had overlooked by concentrating on the car and not the contest.

"It says here that the winner of the season finals will win $2,500 in college scholarships. It doesn't say anything about winning cash."

"Shoot!," Jess said.

"But wait. It goes on to says that area businesses have agreed to match the scholarship amount of $2,500, to be donated to the charitable organization of the winning team's choice," John David continued to read.

"That's it! We could build a car, win the finals and donate the money to Harvey for Sloppy. We could call it the Sumner Junkyard Dog Rescue Fund or something!," Jess said excitedly.

"That only leaves us with three problems. We still need the money to build a car and enter it. We would have to *win* the race. And, it says that to enter in the season finals, you have to qualify with points earned over the entire season. It's kind of late in the season for that," John David said.

"Well, I'm not gonna lose Sloppy, I'm not gonna lose the junkyard, and I'm not gonna lose the race," Jess stated.

Assured by Jess's confidence that they were doing the right thing, the boys pushed on and continued to think of way to get a car built.

Jess's speech alone did not solve their problems. Several minutes later there was a hush from the youngsters again. Then Brian spoke.

"Man, I wish someone would just give us a car. Call Josie and see if her uncle will give us one, too."

"You may be onto something," Jess told him.

"I was joking. No one is gonna just give us a car."

"No, but there is a reason why that car has Frosty's on it. There's a reason why any of them have businesses on them. It's not just because the owners happen to work there. Those people pay to put their names on them for advertising. Sponsors…why didn't we think of that before?"

"I was kind of wanting to have it be the Go-Kart Alley car. But since we don't have any money, I can live with driving someone else's car. Who should we talk to about sponsoring?," Brian asked.

"Well, there's Hawkins Auto Supply or Fred's. I don't think he'd go for it, but there is also Sumner Small Engine. And, as a last resort, there's McCormick Machine," Jess said.

"What do you mean, last resort?," John David asked. "I'd talk to your dad first. He got you started in this business. He'd probably get you started into drag racing."

"I don't know. I wanted us to do this thing ourselves. If we had the family name on the side, people might think my dad built it for me. I'd just rather try someone else first. I'd put my money on Carl at the parts store."

They got a presentation together and made a trip uptown to see Carl. He asked how the go-kart business was going and the boys told him. It wasn't long before they made their ruthless attack for sponsorship. They explained their situation and their intentions.

"Jr. dragsters, huh? I saw one of them just the other day,

over in Sand Flat," Carl said.

"The Frosty's car?," Jess asked, with confidence that Josie's had been the one he had seen.

"No, that wasn't it. I special delivered some parts over there out on that dead-end county road 1850. You know the "Patterson Hood," where all them Patterson boys live out there together. Well, them boys are into racing big time. They're always building drag cars or dirt track cars. The place is full of old cars and trucks. They had one, had it painted up with the name of their truckin' company on the side. The youngest boy drives it down to Bay City," Carl told them.

"Tony?," Jess asked, and then held his breath.

"Yeah, that's it. He's pretty fierce I hear--the leading points winner in the juniors. Of course, I'll bet that's cause his daddy probably beats him if he loses."

"This drag racing deal just gets better and better," Jess said sarcastically. "First I find out my girlfriend drives, now my arch rival. Well, what do you say, do you want us to build the Hawkins Auto Supply dragster and whoop him?"

"Sorry, boys. I wish I could, but I been through the wringer before on drag race sponsorship. Not that I don't have faith in you boys. I'm just still licking my wounds from the big car I sponsored before. Sorry," Carl said.

The boys didn't get too upset. There was still Fred's. They decided not to even bother with Sumner Small Engine, since they probably stole a lot of potential go-kart business from him. But they had given Fred's so much business over the summer, by making it the premier go-kart hangout on the trail, that they were sure he would go for it.

But Fred turned them down as well. He said there were so many kids that came in, he couldn't sponsor just one group. He just didn't want to show any favoritism.

The boys understood and decided to hang around awhile and drown their sorrows in pepperoni grease and Sun-Drop. It was quiet in the restaurant. Too early for lunch, just after the store opened. They were the only ones in the back and the only sound was of a dishwasher running and Fred making their order in the kitchen. Then there were voices.

Someone had come into the kitchen through the side door and was talking to Fred. They could hear glass tinking together and the thud of something heavy being set down.

"You're here early," they heard Fred say followed by the muffled response of the other person coming from a part of the kitchen they couldn't hear.

"Oh, well, they're in there." Fred told the other voice. Shortly they saw who he was talking to.

"I just came from your shop, but you weren't there. I went ahead and left a couple cases outside and picked up your empties. I left the bill stuffed in the door," the man said.

It was Stanley from Teague's Beverage, standing over their booth with his green Sun-drop shirt on. Stanley was the guy who operated the local Sun-drop truck that delivered to their machine at the shop. They were supposed to always be there on Thursday mornings to pay their bill, but this day it had slipped their minds.

"What's the matter with you guys? I looks like you lost your dog or something," he said.

Brian looked at him funny.

"Oh, no. That wasn't it, was it?," Stanley asked as if knowing he had stuck his foot in his mouth.

"Well, kind of," Jess said and proceeded to tell him their predicament.

"Well, did you think about calling Teague's? You know they bottle Sun-drop right in Bay City. It's the only place that still makes it in the returnable bottles. I tell my boss about how much you guys sell out of your little machine, all the time. I even told him all about your shop. He's been wanting to come out and see it, anyway. If I were you, I'd try him. He's loaded," Stanley told them.

The clouds parted and a ray of sunlight shined on the booth. Their problems were over. They had a sponsor. Stanley gave them a business card, and the boss's home phone number as well. They told Fred they needed the pizza to go; they had work to do.

They went to the house to draft a professional proposal to the owner of Teague's Beverage. They wanted to make sure they did this right. Teague's was their last hope before me, and they wanted to do it themselves.

They wrote out everything they wanted to say to the bottling company owner, backed by sound logic and reasoning, along with price quotes on parts, entry fees and the like. They also prepared a list of their qualifications to drive and build small engine race cars, as well as academic and other school achievements. When they had it all planned out, Jess nervously made the call.

Stanley had already tipped off the boss about the boy's trouble. He was expecting the call. He was more enthusiastic than Jess and did most of the talking. Jess barely got a chance to mention half of the things on the list. The owner even made an appointment to come and see their shop that very afternoon.

The others heard Jess being cut off, over and over, in his attempt to give their qualifications and reasoning. They figured he was getting blown off, judging by the dumbfounded look on his face. They approached him cautiously after he hung up the phone.

"Well?," John David asked.

"We got it!," Jess told him.

They all cheered, and Jess filled them in on the visit coming that afternoon. They cleaned up a little, themselves as well as the shop, and got ready to show off all that they could do.

The interview went extremely well, and the owner was very impressed with their work and was glad to see the start they already had on the dragster frame. He always dug go-karts and had many fond memories of them as a kid. He was glad to see some youngsters realizing their potential. They got the Sun-drop sponsorship which came with an almost unlimited budget--unlimited compared to what they were used to working with, which was no budget.

Now, looking through the catalogues wasn't as depressing as it had been earlier in the day. They were setting out to build one bad dragster. New ideas poured onto the table. The only obstacle that stood in their way now, was the fact that the point standing for most of the season had already been established, and there wasn't much time left before the finals. Friday made two weeks until their last chance to compete for points to enter the finals. It still didn't look favorable, even with the new sponsor.

About the time Mr. Teague was visiting with the boys, I was working hard in my office, taking care of paperwork and trying to get caught up around the shop. We were getting behind again, and it was a little hectic.
I was on the phone with a customer and trying to file papers with one hand while adding numbers with the other, juggling it all with the phone held up to my ear by my shoulder. Just then, my shop leadman handed me a slip of paper with some numbers on it.

"My list of PMs, boss," he said, and was out the door as quickly as he came in. I was off the phone shortly, and got the papers put away and the numbers added. I breathed a sigh of relief and sat back, wondering which was next. I knew there was something I needed to be doing. Then I remembered the slip of paper he handed me and uncovered it on my desk.
I read over the list of parts he needed to do that week's preventative maintenance.

I read through the list of part numbers and quantities. Everything seemed normal enough. I set the paper back on my "to do" pile and started to work on something else, but one of the numbers stuck in my head, and I picked up the paper again. I read the number to see if it was the one I was thinking of. I remembered it, because it was expensive. Then I went out into the shop to find the leadman.

"Are you sure we need the filters for the number five mill again. We just changed them three weeks ago," I told him.

"Well, I'll check again, but the hour meter on the machine shows it's logged more time than that...Yep, it's time to change again," he said.

"That's impossible. There is no way we ran that many hours since the last time they were changed," I said.

"Yeah, that does seem funny. But those 426-440-383-005 parts did take a long time to run. Maybe second shift let them run past quittin' time or something. But that still doesn't make sense."

"Yeah, I suppose...Wait a minute. You mean 'dash three,' right?," I asked.

"No. Those hot jobs we ran a couple weeks ago, 'dash five,' with the special cylinder relief," he said.

I had never heard of such a thing.

"I have no idea what you are talking about."

"It was labeled hot. I started making the setup at the end of first shift. Second shift must have finished them up, because they were gone the next day and back on regular production. Don't look at me like that. I had a blueprint and everything."

He went to the filing cabinet to show me the part's print, but it wasn't there.

"And I laid this job out to run?," I asked.

"Well, Jess did. He said you gave it to him to give to me," He said.

"Have there been any other hot jobs that have come through here similar to that?"

He said there were and gave me as many as he could recall. I wrote them on a notepad and went around the shop trying to find other similar stories. I found plenty, especially when second shift arrived.

When I put all of the pieces together, I got in my truck and headed for home. I wanted to hear this whole story.

I pulled up in the yard and began walking hurriedly down to the go-kart shop, where I found the boys working and caught them off guard.

"Dad! Uh, what are you doing home so early?," Jess asked.

"Well, we're getting behind again at the shop, and I was wondering if you would mind coming back to work for a while. We have a whole mess of 426-440-383-005 castings to run, and I thought you could help out," I said, sounding angry.

Jess knew he was in trouble, but didn't know what to do.

"Sure, dad. You know I'll help out anytime you need me," he said hoping that maybe he could play dumb.

"Listen, you! I don't know what's going on here, but I want

to know the story, and I want to know...*what the hell is that!*," I said, changing my tone from angry to bewildered, looking straight at the Deuce.

"Oh...uh...that...it's, uh...it's my new go-kart," Jess said.

"Where in the hell did you get a go-kart like that?," I asked, moving in for a closer look. I started to notice all of the estranged parts that had been altered to run in my shop.

"You built this?," I asked.

"Yeah, I kinda used some scrap from your shop, and I kinda used your employees to help me build it, without them knowing it," he said.

"So I gathered," I said. "But how did you do it right under my nose without me knowing?"

He explained to me how the building of the Deuce went down. He even back tracked to the Heatseeker wreck and filled me in on the events of the entire summer. I was intrigued. I could hardly believe what my kids were able to accomplish with a little bit of imagination and a lot of ingenuity.

It still didn't get him out of trouble, though. I scolded him about working up there alone, and how he could have gotten hurt or crashed a machine. But in the end, I was impressed by the story.

"Wow!," I said, looking around. Then I noticed the dragster frame for the first time. *"Now what the hell is that?"*

Jess continued with his story and let me in on the Jr. dragster plight. The money and Harvey and the whole bit. Even Josie and Tony.

"We'll beat that punk. We can build the fastest dragster out there, and with you at the wheel, we can't lose! Yes, sir, the McCormick Machine car is gonna kick some serious butt!," I told him. He hadn't yet gotten to the part about Teague's Beverage or the Sun-drop sponsorship.

"Well, dad, we kind of already have a sponsor. We wanted to do this ourselves. But we'll still need your help," he told me almost as if he were afraid to burst my bubble.

"Oh. Okay. Well, let me know what you need, and I'll help any way I can," I said after my bubble burst.

They told me about the modifications to the block that would need to be done, as well as the crank and exhaust and intake ports. They also told me about various other things that they did not have the capabilities of doing in their own shop. I agreed to do the work on a contract labor basis, and would only offer suggestions and services. Everything would depend on their say-so.

Chapter 22

They pushed on, working on the car in spite of their one obstacle yet to overcome other than winning the finals. It was on everyone's mind, but they just hoped that everything would work out like the sponsorship did. But Jess knew it wouldn't go away if everyone just ignored it. Finally he broke down and said that it didn't look good. But the guys had faith that he would find a way. So he headed to Sand Flat to visit with Josie's dad about it.

He was obviously well thought of in the Jr. Drag Racing League, and Jess valued his opinion. He wanted to find out their real chances of getting into the finals.

"Ordinarily," he said, "it would be impossible to make it by joining this late in the season. But there might be a slim chance. The point standings have been pretty close this year. Everyone has turned out for record numbers of races, and everyone has had about the same luck. The top four from Bay City Speedway will go into the finals against four from three other area tracks.

The top three spots are pretty well spoken for with Tony Patterson in the lead. But, there is an all out battle for the fourth-place spot. If I can talk to the league, maybe I can see about your team entering with some spotted points. Say with a standing ten points behind last place. It would be a tough battle. I hate to get your hopes up, but technically there is a chance," Mr. Mayfield told him.

That was all that Jess needed to hear. He flew back to the shop and told the others the good news. He lightly mentioned that it would take the League's approval.

They worked with more peace of mind now. The radio played, and the boys worked as a team. Brian had all of his engine specs down, from notes that he had received from Mr. Mayfield, and was ready to head to my shop to get the block bored out, the crank turned down, and the deck plate shaved. He had picked out the best five-horse blocks in the area and had three machined, with two as backups. He did the same for other special made parts.

Parts were coming in overnight delivery, and Mr. Teague was picking up the bill. Jess was back and forth between my shop and his own and Sand Flat, picking up parts and getting advice from everyone he could. He was making drawings at my shop and building parts in both.

It was coming together nicely, but it still had a long way to go. They had very little time to hang out with friends uptown anymore. Most of their friends were coming out to the shop to see what was going on--some of them volunteering to help, just so they could say that they were part of Team Sun-drop.

They had received their sponsorship on Thursday, August 14. They obviously weren't going to be ready for the following Friday's race at Bay City. But they did attend, just to get a better idea of what would go on once they got their car built.

Mr. Mayfield allowed them to be part of the pit crew and get a look at what goes on behind the scenes. They rotated between people helping and people observing from the stands. Someone had to be there with a pad and pencil to write down every time trial, every reaction time, and every race. Jess wanted to know how every round went down, so that he could study it and try not to make the same mistakes as other did.

Sure enough, the leading points winner was on top of his game. Tony never missed a beat. His reaction time was almost always perfect, and he always came within a few thousandths of a second of his dial-in. Tony won the Modified class that night. He was going to be tough to beat. Josie lost in a double breakout in the semifinal round of the Sportsman class.

The league agreed to allow Team Sun-drop to enter under the terms that Josie's dad had set up. They would be spotted just enough points to enter one round behind the low man at the time that they entered. However, they added that Team Sun-drop must, in every round, combat the highest points holder for that round of eliminations. This would make it more fair to the low man who had made it out to every race of the season. There were two more competitions left before the finals. If they could make it to both of those, they might be able to rustle up enough points to take the fourth-place spot going to finals. August 22 and 29 were the last two regular season races, and the finals were on Saturday, August 30.

They missed out on the 22nd race. Brian ran into motor problems. His first one built, he got some bad alcohol fuel and thought the problem was in the carburetor and overadjusted. In the end, he kind of screwed it up, and there was no time to get it together in time for the race. It would have been embarrassing to show up for their first run with a smoker.

There were plenty of other problems, too. They fiberglass body they ordered from a company in Prichard was finished, but there wasn't anyone who could go get it. The glass manufacturer couldn't deliver it, and I was far too busy up at my shop. They called Mr. Teague but he was out of town. The only way they could think to get it home, was to take their little truck and drive nearly fifty miles over motor vehicle prohibited trail.

Jess, John David, Shawn and Brian all piled on the truck and covered up the signs that said Go-Kart Alley. They threw on a few bags of feed from Shawn's place and headed west. Their story was that they were from out of town helping their uncle on his farm and got lost on the farm cart. They had to use it twice. It worked.

This trip could not have come at a worse time. It was a pain in the butt, but they packed a cooler full of Sun-drop and some cold Fred's pizza and made the best of it. After several hours of driving, they finally made it to Prichard to get the body. They tied it down to the overhead rack and laughed and joked all the way back. It wasted an entire precious workday, but it turned out to be a pretty good road trip.

The dragster was just barely assembled on the 22nd, but they had to pull the motor back off to work on it. By the next day, it was built but by no means finished. The body was still just primer colored and many of the tubes and lines were only taped or wired in place. The rulebook stated that these would have to be mounted more securely. But it was good enough to make a trial run.

They had lengthened the trailer out to accommodate the dragster. They loaded the newly built car onto the stretched trailer hitched it to the truck, then hauled it down the backpath to the trail, and unloaded it for its first trial run.

It died a time or two, and the guys had to get it started again. They were not allowed to have a starter mounted on the motor, nor would they want one, because it would add more weight. The modifications made it way too hard to start with a rope. So they made a portable starter by salvaging the starter motor off the Heatseeker and mounting it in a box that also housed a battery. There was a drive socket that attached to the started motor, which coupled to the flywheel. All they had to do was put it up to the flywheel, push the button, and vroom! The powerful modified engine came to life.

A little bit of tuning, and Brian had it to where it didn't die anymore. Jess carefully tested the acceleration and the brakes and steering. When he was sure everything was doing all right, he really pushed it to see what Brian's power plant could do.

It was awesome. Brian had really outdone himself this time. Jess couldn't believe the amount of power that was coming out of the little engine they had rescued from the junkpile.

He made a few runs, and then they tried to time him with a stopwatch, but the times proved to be nonuseful information. With the tight wins and reaction times that they were getting at the track, they needed more accurate times to practice by. But it was enough to get all of the squeaks and rattles out of the car before they handed it over to Roman to paint.

He had the paint scheme all worked out, and they had already run it past Mr. Teague. It was going to be solid light green, almost an olive but brighter, the same color as the bulk of the soda machine. The yellow logo of Sun-drop was to be painted on each side on the tallest part of the body near the driver. The logo is of a teardrop shape, that looks like it is falling down at an angle. Solid yellow in color, broken up around the edges into smaller droplets spraying off. The words, Sun-drop, were written inside the logo in red letters with "Sun-" being over "drop," and the two being at a slightly different angle than the drop itself.

Roman wanted to use those droplets and the angle of the drop into his scheme. He wanted the point of the drop to angle toward the back of the car, as if being blown by the wind. Then he wanted to make the small spray of droplets to become a larger spray on the backside. Kind of like painting flames on a car, but with Sun-drop soda drops, instead. He planned to add a little of the same coming off the nose. The frame and roll bars were going to be the same red as the lettering.

While Roman went to work, Jess and Brian came to see me. I had called them and told them to bring their truck. I had some old junk to get rid of and, if they didn't come get it, I would throw it out. They really didn't believe me, but they figured something must be up, so they came down anyway. When they got there, they saw through my surprise.

I had a little present for them from the guys at the shop. They all pitched in to build them a portable staging tree. We worked with a lot of electronic equipment in some of the machines we built, many using electric eyes. So, with our combined skills, we built a tree that would figure reaction time and elapsed time for one lane, and we showed them how it worked.

They immediately took it down to the trail to set it up. The trail authority would probably frown on them using it as a drag strip, so they did it incognito. They set short posts on either side of the trail; one side with mounting plates screwed to them, the others with reflectors on them. They buried the wires in the loose crushed ballast on the sides of the pavement of the trail.

When they needed it, and the trail was deserted, they just set up the tree and attached the electric eyes to the mounting plates in their proper, premeasured positions and attached the wires. Then Jess was ready to practice his reaction times and nailing the dial-in every time. He couldn't do it at first, but he never gave up. He practiced and practiced to where Brian had to pull the spark plug wire off and force him to let the motor cool down.

The car looked sharp all painted and shined up. They had received all of their safety equipment now, and Roman had even put a good airbrush job on the helmet. Jess had a rush, looking down the gleaming green paint job, reflecting the tall pine trees on either side of the trail. He saw the reflection of the lights on the tree flash down to green, as he cut a perfect light with a .500 reaction time. There were no gears to shift in this car. It was equipped with a high-dollar torque converter, that was designed to always be in the right gear at the right time. All Jess had to do was put the pedal to the metal and look for the win light. Everyone had at least one turn in the cockpit, but everyone agreed that it was pretty much Jess's car.

Mr. Teague was glad to hear that they had finished the car and that practice was going so well. He came out to see it and was truly impressed, as was I. He congratulated me on raising such fine boys. Although, seeing what all they had done without me, I'm not sure how much I really had to do with it.

The last chance to qualify was only a few days away. Missing the 22nd race hurt their chances pretty bad. The only chance they had of winning now, was if one of the top points winners didn't show up, not needing the points of the 29th race anyway. Still, they would have to win every round to gain enough points to pass even the last place guy ahead of them. In addition to having to win every single round, they would always be up against the toughest competitor in every round. It would be tough. Jess had heard it plenty of times leading up to the race, but he was up for the challenge.

The portable staging tree was working great, but Jess figured that he had better get used to the actual track. Mr. Mayfield said that sometimes it can make a difference as to which track you were at, or even which lane. Wednesday night, he made a return trip to the racing school to get in some trial runs on the track prior to Friday's race.

It was a good thing that they did attend, because there was a difference between practicing on the trail and at the track. The biggest difference was the amount of rubber on the track.

The car got different traction on the well broken-in racetrack than over the practically brand new trail. It changed his reaction time as well as his elapsed time. He didn't want to change his system, so Brian adjusted the idle of the engine to compensate for the traction change on reaction time.

Jess developed a technique of taking off without redlighting. He broke the last yellow light up into three stages, coming on, on, and going off. He tried to leave while it was going off. He perfected his time by keeping an Engine Joe song stuck in his head while staging. When the first yellow light came on, it would trigger a certain part of the song that went with the lights counting down. By the time the last yellow was coming on, the song in Jess' head was in time with the light, and he punched it on a cymbal crash. It worked well on the trail, and once Brian had adjusted the idle, it worked just as well at the track.

The Wednesday's track trip was the smartest thing they could have done. It had given them much valuable information that they needed if they were going to win on Friday. Without it, they would have put the car on the trailer after the first round.

Chapter 23

Race day was upon them. Friday morning, they were in the shop around nine. Jess wanted to get plenty of rest, but not so much that he was groggy. He ate a healthy breakfast to give him a good energy boost. There was plenty to do, in preparation for that night, to help him burn it off.

Roman put some finishing touches on the car. He added all of the minor sponsors and names of people the team wanted to thank. The people who had turned down the major sponsorship still contributed, and the boys wanted to give them a spot on the paint. Some were stickers, and some Roman painted himself. Fred's and Hawkins Auto Supply made it on and, of course, so did McCormick Machine. Along the side of the car, in small yellow lettering, were people's names, which included Mr. Mayfield, moms and dads, and Harvey and Sloppy.

Jess's favorite was the sticker that Engine Joe had given him. It had their name and a catch phrase from a new song they had written. It said "Everything You Thought Was Right Was Wrong Today." Jess thought the phrase was entirely too fitting for other people's responses to their chances at winning the finals.

The final touch Roman put on was an old, old Sun-drop logo. They had found it on one of the bottles that came through from back when it was called Sun-drop Golden Cola. It was very cool looking, like something you would see on a World War II fighter plane. The logo was two golden yellow rings, one inside the other, with lettering in between the inside and outside ones. At the top it said "First For Thirst," with "since 1930" underneath. The bottom of the two said the name of the original bottling company. Inside the center was a golden-haired young woman in a golden yellow two-piece bathing suit, sitting in a teacup with "Golden cola" written on it in golden yellow cursive letters. Her legs and feet, adorned with golden high heel shoes, were hanging out of the cup and extended out of the rings. In front of her, was a bottle of Sun-drop Golden Cola.

Jess was readying the cockpit. First, he put up a picture of Harvey and Sloppy sitting under his awning, along with one of the gang snapped out in front of the Go-Kart Alley shop. He also put up, from his wallet, the small school photo that Josie gave him. An extra sticker of Engine Joe's so he could see the catch phrase, and he was ready for the final touch. He took the T-handled shift lever out of the Heatseeker and mounted it alongside his seat. Even though it served no useful purpose, it was there as a reminder of what all he had learned that summer.

They did all the preparing they could do, followed by some relaxing. When the day waned to afternoon, they decided to head to the track early. Then they trailered the car, and packed up everything that they thought they might need in the way of tools, parts, food and drinks. The truck was full and so was any extra space on the trailer. They did not want to come ill-prepared. Everyone took their own go-karts except Brian and John David, who rode on the truck. They were sent off by an entourage of well-wishers as they pulled off the backpath onto the trail. Many followed to root them on to victory.

They got to the track early and staked out a pit area under a clump of shade trees. They would need it, for it was a sultry summer afternoon and wouldn't cool off until the sun went down. They unloaded the car and organized their supplies. Brian gave the motor a test start-up and made sure it was running all right.

More cars started to arrive, big as well as juniors. Soon the whole area set aside for pits was filled with one-ton pickup trucks, campers, trailers and race cars; with everyone unloading their cars and making test fires. Spectators began to arrive as well, and the place was filling up.

Jr. dragsters were set to make their time trials first, followed by big car trials and beginning big car eliminations. Junior racing came in the middle, followed by the wrap-up of the big cars.

The boys wandered around, looking at all of the different junior cars. Many cars were back from the last race they had seen. The boys were looking for three in particular--the top three in the point standing; Tony's, especially. There were a lot of Jr. drag racers there. Shawn counted about twenty-eight, but he never saw Tony's.

When it came time to make the trials, the announcer welcomed the spectators and racers alike and made first call for Modified juniors to come to the staging lanes. The boys gathered their stuff and pushed the car to the lanes. All of the cars arrived and they were able to get a good look at who was in attendance. As it turned out, luck was on their side; none of the top three point holders had come out. They were so far ahead, there was no way any of the others could surpass third place. The only thing left in the way of going to finals now, was the simple problem of winning what looked to be five rounds of fierce competition.

The cars inched forward, with drivers suiting up and taking the wheel. Fathers and family members walked with them, helping them along the way. Systematically, they paired up and waited for their chance to go. Crew chiefs started the cars and escorted them around the corner of the fence, around the tower and onto the track.

When one set of cars had taken off, the crew chief of the next pair would signal their drivers to do a burnout and warm up the tires and such. Then they would monkey with the engine, adjusting the idle, then help them stage. When they were staged, the lights went down, and the two cars were gone, leaving an opening for the next pair.

The boys felt lost. They had been in the pits before, but it all seemed weird and confusing now that they had their own car. Luckily, Mr. Mayfield helped coach them through the process, and it seemed a little more familiar with him around. Brian tried to look like he knew as much as the other crew chief's. As he escorted Jess onto the track, he had to zone out the surroundings to concentrate on his skills. In the end, Jess made it through his first session pretty well, with a .527 second reaction time and an E.T. of 8.222 seconds at a top speed of 78.25 mile per hour. Not too bad. Second round yielded a .503 reaction time, 8.236 E.T., at 78.83 mph.

Jess parked the car back near their trailer and unsuited. When the guys made it back, they reviewed Jess's record of matching his dial-in and his two E.T's for the night. With some advice from their veteran friend, they agreed on a dial-in for the elimination races.

The guys talked to several of the other kids racing Jr. dragsters. Some even came by to check out their car and wish them luck. It may have been because they didn't see Jess's and the guys' team as a threat, with their low experience and kid-built car. If so, they didn't realize the amount of resources the guys had at their disposal. But overall, it sure seemed like everyone was friendly and in the best interest of fun.

They wandered up to watch the big cars, but Jess didn't stay long. He tried to pace the butterflies out of his stomach, back at the car. Josie came to visit and give him some reassurance. She tried her best, but she was new at this, too, and wasn't facing the same challenge as he. Her voice soothed him just the same. She could have been talking about moon rockets, and it would have made him feel just as good.

When it got to be "Go Time," the announcer made a call for first round eliminations, Modified class juniors. Instantly, the butterflies surged in Jess's stomach again. The rest of the crew came up and helped him get started on his way to the staging lanes.

All of the cars for the first round were paired up, and assigned lanes randomly by drawing number cards from a deck. All except the highest points holder and Jess, they were held back to run against each other. Two by two, they left the lanes until the only two left were the Sun-drop car and a dark blue car with white flames and no visible sponsor. Then it was time to fire up.

Their powerful modified engines roared to life and the two surged around the corner onto the track. Jess knew the procedure and made his burnout to warm up. He stopped just before the starting line, and Brian pushed him back for another burnout. Then Brian pointed out when his car was almost even with the first staging beam. He then backed out of the way and let Jess take over.

When he was staged up in the right lane, he knew it was very important that he stay focused, for it would only be a second or two before he was flagged off. It was hard to do, because his hands were tingling with so much excitement that he could barely feel the wheel. He gripped tighter, trying to stay in control.

His dial-in was posted on the car, and the track men entered it along with his opponent's, into the computer. They were posted on the lighted billboards at the other end, and Jess could see that his opponent would have the head start. The lights went down, and his opponent took off, roaring loudly.

Jess tried to keep the song in his head, but it didn't sound the same. Only one part repeated over and over like a broken record. He tried to focus, to the point where he felt like closing his eyes but couldn't, then the first yellow light came on. The song fell into place, and he hit the gas right on the cymbal crash. It felt early to Jess, and his first thought was that he was going to see a red light, but he didn't. It was green, and he stayed on the gas and sped towards his leading opponent. He kept the pedal down and focused on the end of the track.

The one advantage that Jess had failed to realize about bracket racing was, that if the other car has a head start, there is a tremendous thrill in overtaking it before the finish line. As he came up on the tail end of the white flame car he felt an adrenaline rush that flourished on top of the nerves that had already been electrified by the start of the race. With the sight of the finish line rapidly approaching, and the other car looking like he might get there first, it made a cruelly close finish. But Jess just kept gaining on top of his gain and soon overtook the other car and took the win light by a few feet.

With a perfect reaction time of .500 seconds and an E.T. dangerously close to their dial, Team Sun-drop wowed the crowd, as well as other racers. Jess didn't hear a word of it because of the tense situation and the loud motors at the starting line, but the others told him that the announcer gave a little rundown of Team Sun-drop and the night's underdog fight to make it to the finals. Their performance made it look as though they were underestimated as an inexperienced team. They bumped up several notches with some of the eliminations made over round one.

The Sportsman class round one eliminations ran next. While they waited to be called to run again in round two, Modified, Jess and Brian talked about the reaction time and the motors performance. Jess said the motor did fine, it was his jumpiness that got the reaction time so low. They also decided the dial was OK, too, and left it alone. The call came, and they headed back to the staging lanes.

Again they were pitted against the top car, as the others filed away, and soon they took the lanes. The other car, sponsored by a body shop and painted with long, tapered orange and black stripes, was a little more concerned than his first opponent had been and stared down the Sun-drop car. The driver respected the fact that Jess showed that he was good, but set out to prove his inexperience.

He was a little too anxious to teach. The two had similar dial-ins and took off only a fraction of a second apart. Jess could see, as he took off, that his opponent had a red light in contrast to his own green. It was an automatic win, but he still ran it as a competition for practice.

There were much fewer cars now as they neared round three and the cycle back to the starting line was much shorter. Jess was a little more confident now that he had won some. The tingling in his hands lessened as he staged for round three. He barely paid any attention to the checkered flag painted car next to him. He was in a groove and concentrated on winning.

This round, Jess had the head start. He rolled up and staged with confidence, the song playing very clearly in his head despite all of the noise and waving of spectators. He was thinking how much better it felt than the first round, and how it was not nearly as hard as he thought. Just then his lights were going down, and he realized he had begun daydreaming right there in the middle of competition. In shock, he tried to get back on track and did so too quickly. The red light was as bright as a spotlight shining in his eyes.

Jess couldn't believe it. He'd blown it. He got too cocky and blew it for Harvey and Sloppy, for Teague's Beverage and me, for the gang and all of the spectators rooting for the underdog. Harvey and Sloppy seemed to stare up at him from the picture saying "Oh, well. You did your best." But Jess couldn't accept what they had to say, he knew he had screwed up.

He pushed on just the same. It was the end of his season, but not the end of his career. He would need the information sometime. He had heard that you could never have enough time trials. He reached the end of the track and let off the accelerator. He looked at his time, and it was good; he wouldn't have broken out. He expected the other car to come around a lot sooner than it did but it finally came around. He figured the other driver took it easy since he had a free round.

Right before he went past the billboard, Jess noticed something odd. The win light was posted on his side. He figured it was a mistake and headed on to the trailer.

He was getting out and pulling off his helmet, when the others came out running and cheering.

"What are you carrying on about? We lost," Jess said.

"The other car had a steering problem and crossed the center line!," John David said.

"So. I red lighted; the rulebook. The worst rule you can break is crossing the centerline, even worse than a foul start. That means you won!," John David yelled.

The wheels in Jess's head began to turn, sorting out this new information.

"We're still in the game?," he asked, getting excited.

"We're going to the semifinal round. Just two more races, and it's on to the finals!"

Jess began jumping up and down, body slamming with the football player, hugging and cheering with the crew. Brian broke up the celebrating by pointing out Jess's little bout of overconfidence in the last round, that nearly ruined them by a red light. He quickly came down from excitement and concentrated. Brian handed him his helmet and instructed the crew to get the car down to the staging lanes.

Once again Jess was paired up with the top competitor and sent in to do battle. He had the head start again, and it made him nervous. It was a good thing. Apparently, Jess focused better under pressure. He jumped on the tree with caution this time, but still kept a good reaction time. He was off down the track, with the other car chasing soon after.

Jess held the pedal down and payed close attention to his car's performance. He was not sure, but it felt a little faster than normal. Out of fear of breaking out, he let off just a little but got worried and pushed it back down.

The other car began to overtake him and was closing in on the finish line. In a flash, the lights tripped and the other car crossed the line first, followed by Jess who captured the win light. His opponent had broken out, in an attempt to take Jess out in the semifinal round. That win alone would have been enough to secure him the fourth-place spot for the season final race. But his greed made him push it a little too far.

They took a short breather to let their motors cool while the final round of Sportsman class ran. Jess hadn't had a chance to keep up with Josie's progress. He learned that she lost to a good friend in the third round, due to an intentional red light. The point standing for Sportsman class was not as close as Modified. With her large absence from the track that season, she had no chance of winning, and her friend needed the points. So she let her win, which was a nice gesture, for her friend ended up winning the final round.

Then they could wait no more. It was time to do the final battle. Jess and Team Sun-drop had come from dead last, all the way up to a tie for second place in this last competition for the finals. The one that Jess had just beaten was in first place. Just entering in the final round for Jess and his opponent was enough to tie him. That guy's only hope would be for a double red light in the final round. Then there would be a three-way tie, which would have to be settled by some sort of sudden death match. It was highly unlikely, but with the intensity in the air, anything was possible.

With the winning of the final round, came the bonus points needed to move on to the finals. Both cars wanted it badly and both were sharp as razors. They focused hard and tried not to make any previous near-mistakes affect this race.

Their dial-ins were very close, and Jess would take off second, the way he preferred it. Jess's song was loud and clear--louder than any other thought or daydream he could have had. Even the other driver's acceleration during Jess's lights didn't throw it off. It was in perfect time with the lights.

With a pair of green lights, they battled in an all out fight for the finals. Both were relentless to beat the other and showed no mercy.

The same as in the last race, he noticed the car going faster than before. He hadn't changed his dial-in after the last race or even mention it to anyone for that matter. Not knowing what to do, he decided to let off just before the finish line. As the other car tripped his lights first, Jess wondered if he had done the right thing. The win light in his lane assured him that he did. It was a double breakout race, but Jess had let off just enough to keep himself closer to his dial. This time Harvey smiled at him from the picture, saying, "Good job!"

Jess was greeted by tons of fans as he pulled up to the trailer. The guys were shaking up bottles of Sun-drop and spraying it all over him and the car. Even Mr. Teague was in on the action. Jess shook hand after hand, graciously accepting the congratulations. Even their toughest competitors of the evening gave them credit on a job well done; pulling off what they, admittedly, thought was impossible. I wish my wife and I could have been there to congratulate him, too; him and Brian both, but we stayed away at the request of the team. Jess thought he would be too nervous if he knew his mother and I were there.

They didn't hang around too long after their win. It was a long drive home, and they needed their rest for an even bigger day following. Brian led the pack with the truck and its big front headlights. Jess rode with him and gave the Deuce up to John David, for he wanted to talk with his little brother, business partner, and crew chief on the ride home. Ordinarily, they would have spent this night in agony, dreading the passing of the last weekend of summer. But they had too much else to think about, and it never crossed their minds.

Chapter 24

Jess and Brian had a good visit on the long ride along the lonely, dark stretch of trail. Shawn turned off at his house between Sand Flat and the old iron gate. Roman kept heading for home, as Jess, Brian, and John David turned up the backpath to the shop.

I was anxiously waiting for them to return. They were busy unloading and putting everything away, when we got out to the shop. I helped them finish, as they told us their tale of racing victory.

The next morning, they were up at early and rolling the car out into the sunlight. They took a hose and rag to wash off all of the sticky Sun-drop that had been sprayed all over it the night before. Then gave it a good wax job, making it slick and shiny again.

Brian fired it up and did some test tuning. Jess climbed in and made sure all of the controls were free and working well. Then they sat around reviewing their time slips and the round by round results from the race. They also thought about all the supplies they had taken to the track. There was a lot of supplies they hadn't used, and they wondered if they really needed it for their return trip.

The only real engine work Brian really had to do all night, was adjusting the idle a little. For the most part, it was a self-sufficient car. They talked about taking only minimal supplies but, in the end, decided to take them all.

Meanwhile, Tony was learning of the race results. When he found out Jess and the guys came up from dead last, winning every single round, he couldn't believe it. He heard they were entering a car but wasn't the least bit worried about them actually making it out of the first one or two rounds. Tony's dad was plenty upset when he found out, as well. He was angry for Tony's opting to back out of the last competition race. They began pulling out all of the stops on his car, and Tony was instructed not to lose, especially to some amateurs, no matter what.

Jess took the car down to the trail for a few burnouts. He didn't want to take the practice tree, because there was a big difference from the track to the trail. He didn't want to affect his performance, feeling it would be best to keep his experiences from the track fresh on his mind. The car was still running great, and he was satisfied enough to take it back to the shop.

They loaded up the car and supplies early and rested until about noon. Then they set out on one last trek to Bay City Speedway, where the first annual Jr. Dragster Area Finals were to be held. They had to leave earlier this time, because it was going to be a big day of racing at the track. The juniors were going to run their eliminations in rotation with the big cars.

They were there early again and took their same pit under the shade trees. One big car team took a spot next to the guys and rolled out their 1968 Dodge Charger drag car. The boys admired its powerful muscle car look, and the owners enjoyed showing it off. They had been there the night before and knew of the boy's story. The boys received good luck wishes and an open invitation to anything they might need from the Dodge owners' trailer.

Tony was at the track soon after the boys, with his brothers and cousins, dad and uncles, unloading cars and tools, lawn chairs and beer coolers. Jess could tell the Patterson clan was talking about him, because they stared right at him while they did.

Josie and her dad were at the track and came over to say "Hello." The boys were busy getting all of their stuff arranged and making sure they were ready. Josie talked with Jess as he carried off toolboxes, motor parts, and gas cans.

Someone else had shown up, whom the boys hadn't seen in several weeks. Zack actually drove out in his demon kart and came to help out Tony. He parked by Tony's trailer and got out to greet his family.

"Those two together again? You better watch out, Jess," Shawn said.

"Well, I don't see any big hills around, and I don't think

anything can roll through the guard rails and onto the track. So maybe I'm safe this time," Jess replied.

The place filled in quickly, in anticipation of a big night of racing. There had to have been twice as many people and cars there as the previous night. There were food vendors and parts booths set up everywhere, and the air was filled with excitement.

The boys got the car ready, and Jess got suited up. The Junior time trials were to run first again, and they wanted to be ready. Jess looked around the busy field full of cars and trailers and took a deep breath.

When the announcer made the call for the first session of time trials, they pushed the car up to the staging lanes, staying on the other side from Tony. They weren't afraid of him, but it would be awkward to be right next to him, with his motley family and Zack hanging around.

There were thirty-two cars in all, sixteen from Sportsman and sixteen from Modified. Four from each class were there, from four area tracks. All of the places were filled, and there would be no bye runs in this race.

These cars were the baddest of the bad. Every car looked its best and held a motor and driver to back up it's good looks. They were surrounded in a sea of chrome and racing stripes, checkered flags and proud sponsor logos. The Sun-drop car fit right it. Roman even added, for intimidation, some little black dragsters right next to their pinup gal; one for every round they had won.

The first pair to run, fired up and headed onto the track for their trial run. Tony ended up in the second round, and Jess was in the third. When Tony pulled up to make his burnout, three family members were with him in the lane--his dad, an older brother, perhaps, and maybe an uncle.

His dad was very bossy and had a surly look on his face as he walked out. He pointed down the track, forcefully signaling the burnout. About the time the car got going, he yelled at Tony to stop and grabbed the roll bars right as he did, pushing it back for another burnout. He made wild hand motions and barked orders. He was moving recklessly around the moving car, nearly getting his toes run over as he went in to adjust the engine. Jess was glad he had a crew chief that had some faith in his ability to burnout and stage a car.

Tony sped off and received an impressive reaction time of .502 with an elapsed time of 7.931 and a top speed of 80.80 mph. Zack was waiting inside the guardrail and met Tony's family as they walked off to get Tony's time slip.

Jess knew his car was running faster as the previous night went on, but he had no idea how much. His first time trial proved just how much. His first reaction time was a little quick, a .498 with an increased E.T. of 8.046 and a top speed of 79.94 mph. Brian didn't know why the car was doing this, but Jess didn't knock it, because it was running smooth.

Tony's second run stayed very close to his first run, as did Jess's. Jess changed his reaction to .505 and almost matched his first run E.T. with an 8.032 and a top speed of 79.98 mph.

All of the cars were fast, and all of the drivers were sharp. Most of the winning in this race would end up being green light starts with heads-up finishes. This time their toughest competition would no longer be a bunch of fourth-place contenders, but experienced warriors, with many more tricks up their sleeves.

All of the gang was gathered under their shade tree getting ready for eliminations. Jess knew exactly what his dial would be, an even 8.00. They wanted to make sure everything went smoothly and no ground was lost due to poor preparation. Jess knew what he had to do, nail the tree and take the line.

There was what seemed like a long time before the first Junior race. When the call finally came, Jess got the same pinging surge in the pit of his stomach as he had felt before. They rolled up to the lanes and were first in line to go. Jess was paired up by flash card and took his lane. He made his burnouts and the frame rattled under him in a soothing rhythm of power. He staged and got his reaction method cued up again.

He had a slight head start in this round, and even though he preferred going second, he felt good about it. His lights flashed and he took off, the first Junior of the evening to fire off from the starting line. He had no way of knowing what his reaction time was, but he knew it was dead on and the green was shining his way. He was already in front of the other car, and he just had to keep it that way. He did, and the win light was on his side as he trailered the Prichard Raceway representative in the first round.

It was a big relief to get at least one round out of the way. Jess wasn't so much overconfident, as he was collected. He knew a little more about what he was doing, and the car was running fine. He had a good feeling about the night, even if his opponents were tougher. But, as always in drag racing, his toughest competition was going to be himself.

When he got back to the trailer, the guys were running out frantically. He barely came to a stop before Brian practically jumped on top of the engine, and the others hovered around, too. Jess got out and pulled off his helmet, trying to find out what was going on.

"You didn't see it!," Brian shouted.

Just then Jess looked back to see a trail of fading smoke that came from the path he had just made.

"You started smoking just before the end of that round," Brian told him. "It looked bad. We need to find the problem quick!"

Jess took off his jacket and jumped in to look as well. Brian found a trail of oil leaking from near the area where the crankcase meets the cylinder. It was evident that it had been blowing out onto the hot exhaust pipe. Grabbing a rag and wiping it clean it, they could see a stress crack was forming in the casting, just below the cooling fins.

Upon closer inspection, it didn't look too bad. It didn't leak when the motor was idling, only when they revved it up. Brian decided it was only happening at high rpm's and shouldn't affect performance, if they could get it stopped.

Jess thought quick and pulled a tube of Shoe Goo from his toolbox. He kept it for adhering fasteners and things to frames, where he couldn't weld or screw them. They cleaned and degreased the crack. Then they squeezed the sticky stuff from the tube all over it. Dobbing it around, it looked like they would get a good seal. They let it cure for a minute and fired the engine. Even at high rpm's the oil remained in the crankcase.

With the problem solved, they waited for the next round. Jess didn't let it bother him, because he was sure the Shoe Goo would do the trick. The call came for round two Modified eliminations, and the new group returned for another shot at the top. The Sun-drop car was in the third pair, followed by Tony in the fourth after Jess.

They inched up until the first two pairs had gone, then Brian started their motor. Jess rolled around the tower and took the left lane opposite a black and green car sponsored by Regan Logging.

They got staged with Jess second to go. He had heard the announcer mention his opponent being the highest points holder for his home track. It goes to show, even the best can make mistakes, for the Regan Logging car had a red light giving Jess a free round. As usual Jess treated this round as serious as any other and ran it as hard as he could.

About halfway down the track is when the Sun-drop team's luck took a downturn. The car began sputtering and slowed considerably. Jess's legs tensed--he knew what the problem was. As soon as he rounded the corner coming off the track, he saw a large cloud of gray and black smoke following him. He got it back to the trailer as quickly as he could, and immediately jumped out to inspect the crack.

He wiped it clean and saw that the Shoe Goo did not hold up and, what's worse, the crack had grown considerably in length. The cylinder was literally trying to separate from the crankcase. The engine didn't stand a chance of holding out three more rounds. Fear came over the whole team.

Brian only fretted for a moment, for he knew the only solution, and there wouldn't be much time to do it. The block was no good, and it had to be replaced. He quickly grabbed for some tools and began taking bolts loose. Jess knew it, too, and began removing bolts that Brian had broken loose.

Brian kept breaking them loose, and Jess kept taking them out. The Dodge owners saw what was happening and ran an air hose over from their gas-powered compressor, along with a 3/8- drive power ratchet.

Round three would be coming up soon and, deep in their minds, they wondered if there was even a chance that they could do it in time. Just then there was an accident out on the track. No one was hurt, but one car got messed up. A big car lost its drive- shaft just off the line, which caused it to slam into the guardrail and turn back across the track. In the process, its automatic transmission was busted and oil had gone everywhere on the track. It had to be shut down, while crews tried to clean up the spill.

The power tools sped up the process tremendously. John David, Shawn and Roman handed the tools to Brian and Jess, who were working like mad on the engine, taking it loose. Shortly, they had it off, and the two were carrying it over to the back of the little truck. They set it in a shallow sheet-metal pan and went right back to work. There was no time to wait on the oil to drain; they broke the crankcase cover off, and the hot, black engine contents puked out into the pan. The boys were dirty and getting dirtier, but they didn't slow a bit.

Brian had the head off, and Jess began pushing the piston out the top of the cylinder. Brian caught it with a ring compressor, in an attempt to keep the rings in the same location they had been in on the piston. It wasn't long, and the whole thing was torn down.

The old engine they were running was good and broke in at the point of the failure. The inside of the cylinder was smooth and worn to fit the piston. They feared the new block they would put the piston into, would be too tight and not run well. The Dodge owners brought out a cylinder hone and an air drill, to try and polish the new block sleeve some.

They worked feverishly, looking over their shoulders at every chance to be sure the crew was still working on the track.

When they finally got it back together, the crew was wrapping up on the track cleanup. There was no time for test firing, they had to mount the engine onto the frame as soon as it was together. The guys took over mounting it and hooking up the drivetrain. Jess dug out the notebook I had made for them, from his toolbox, and began quickly turning through the pages. When he found what he was looking for, he took out a pencil and started making marks.

Just as Shawn pulled his wrench away from the last bolt, Brian hit the starter and the engine fired and died. Brian began making all kinds of adjustments right away. It was nervous work, and his hands moved like a magician doing a trick. John David picked up the starter and ran it at Brian's request.

"Hit it!," he would shout. John David would try. And if it didn't start, "Wait!," he shouted again.

This went on several times, until the engine finally fired and ran. Brian tuned the carburetor and revved the engine, trying to get it to sound as good as the one before. He did his best.

About the time he got it up and going, Jess moved in with his notebook. Brian revved up the engine and tried to find the max rpm's. He showed the results from the tachometer to Jess, who immediately began pencil-whipping the numbers in the notebook.

There was no time, nor would they even get a chance, for another trial run. This was a new motor, and they had no idea how it would run to even set their dial in. Their only hope, was to get the maximum rpm's, calculate them into the gear ratio of the torque converter, and estimate the elapsed time over the eighth mile.

Jess did his best job with the numbers and equations. Even though they had worked on the Heatseeker and the Deuce, they were still just a rough guess. He came up with a 7.90, the fastest time allowed in Jr. Drag Racing. Brian looked at it and whistled. It looked too fast to Jess, too, so he slowed it by five hundredths, making it a 7.95.

Brian agreed, and they put it on the car. By this time, they were making second call for round three Modified. They moved the car quickly back to the staging lanes, in fear they would be disqualified for not showing up on time.

Tony was at the front. He and Zack had been watching the

show over at the guys' trailer and were heckling them the whole time. They were disappointed to see the car make it back to the lanes.

Tony was relentless; he made every round nearly perfect with low reaction times and E.T.'s close to his dial. He went in the round before Jess this time, and once again, took the win.

Jess felt all the butterflies of his very first race. He had no idea if the dial was right, and the idle seemed all too different from his first engine. He was afraid of a red light.

Jess didn't pay any attention to the car next to him. His mind was whirring with thoughts. He wasn't even sure if he should use his normal method of jumping the tree. By the time the lights came on, he just went with his gut and reacted cautiously, leaving when it felt right. It's a good thing, because the Engine Joe song might have caused a red light.

He was in the green and off down the track, chasing the other car. The dial issue scared him to death. The number seemed too fast, but so did the new motor. The other car was screaming down the track, and Jess tried to catch him. It was gonna be close if it worked out right, but Jess was starting to feel like he lost. If he pushed too hard and his guess was too slow, he could break out or even be disqualified for running under 7.90. If it was right and he didn't, he could lose the line. His gut, again, told him to push it.

His gut was right. The other car took the line with a breakout, and Jess nearly nailed his educated guess dial-in with a 7.955. It was such a relief to see the win light.

Chapter 25

Two rounds to go, Jess talked to his crew chief about the new motor's performance. He felt the run went good and only wanted to change the dial to a 7.92. The idle is what he was most concerned with. Jess liked his system and wanted to keep it. He remembered, in crisp detail, how much faster it seemed to have been than the other motor. Brian made the adjustments, and they felt prepared for the next round.

It was the semifinal round. There were only four cars left. Two were contenders from two other tracks, and two were from Bay City Speedway. They were, of course, Jess and Tony. Jess got another surge of nerves as he watched the man draw lane numbers from the deck, assigning the cars to their opponents. He didn't want to be up against Tony, not now. It was all coming to a head and, for the first time, Jess wasn't sure if he could beat Tony. He wanted to put it off one more round, hoping Tony would break out or something.

The lane came up for Jess, and it wasn't opposite Tony. He breathed a sigh of relief for that. But he was still just as nervous about his opponent. Anyone who made it this far had to be good. It was probably as rare as his Deuce engine, that anyone else could have had the bizarre streak of luck that Jess had been having.

At the tree, Jess thought about his song and felt the motor surging. It felt right, almost as the old one did, it must have been getting broken in. It was back to normal, when Jess hit the pedal on the cymbal crash again, and pulled off another .505 reaction time.

He had the lead on the other car off the line, but he was gaining fast. Both cars gave it all they had. Soon they were neck and neck, and it looked as if it could be anyone's race. An all too familiar feeling came over Jess as they neared the line. Jess may not have been used to the new engine, but he knew the car and how it felt under him. He had a flashback to the final race of the night before, and suddenly, knew he was about to breakout. At the last minute, he held up and let the other car take the line.

It was another double breakout, with Jess coming in just .005 under his dial. He didn't know if he was getting good at this or if it was all luck. If it was, he hoped it held out for one more round. He pulled in to his trailer to meet an enthusiastic crew.

When the last round of the semifinals was over, they knew who they would battle for the scholarship and the charity money. It was none other than Tony Patterson, in his R & B Trucking car.

Jess told Brian that he thought the motor was breaking in good, and how he had to let up to keep his breakout down. They agreed on the 7.90 dial-in for the final race. Brian put it on the car with shoe polish, and they waited for the final round.

It was a horrible wait. Jess wished they could go right away, but it was in the plan to hold off for a while and build suspense. It was getting to the point that he didn't care whether he won or lost, he just wanted his nerves to calm down.

My wife and I snuck in just before the semifinal round. We had to be careful to not let any of the crew see us; we didn't want to make Jess nervous. We found a place in good view of the starting line, and if we stretched our necks a little we could see the trailer and the boys' go-karts. I could see Jess pacing around by his car, swinging his hands back and forth, clapping them in the front.

The announcement came for the two finalists to make their way to the staging lanes. As they did, the announcer gave a rundown on each team, including their accomplishments and what charity they were racing for. He included a little story about Sloppy and the junkyard.

When he was done, the two cars fired up and proudly rounded the corner onto the track. Everyone cheered when they came into view. The crowd responded, even more, to the powerful burnouts.

As they began to stage, Jess noticed, for the first time, Tony's dial-in. It was a 7.90, too. It was strange because he hadn't changed his dial all night. It seemed funny that in the last race he would, and to the lowest one possible. Even more peculiar, was that it matched Jess's exactly.

Jess pretty much knew he was in no danger of breaking out, but he wondered about Tony. Did he have a trick up his sleeve? Was his car capable of going a lot faster than he dialed? Maybe he had been dialing purposely low all night, putting along until the last moment, then taking the line by a few inches.

When they were burning out, Jess remembered back to the time he had raced Tony in the Heatseeker on the trail. He had no problems beating him then, but this was a totally different game. Tony's go-kart was just stock, and he thought he had the right gears to race. Jess had much more horsepower and a two-speed transmission. Also, it didn't look like anyone had spent much time on Tony's go-kart; nothing like what had been done to his dragster. Jess imagined that everyone in Tony's racing family must have had a part in tricking out that little five-horse.

Jess couldn't be sure about Tony. All he knew, was that he believed his own dial to be accurate. The only thing he could do, was try to win it at the tree.

Both lanes were staged, and the crowd was on the edge of their seats. Jess stared down the long straight track, lined with hundreds of anxious spectators. The reflection of the lights of the tree, and the stands full of people, on his car, brought back the memory of when he first staged on the trail, and it gave him a good feeling.

Soon the yellow lights were coming on and going off and the heads up race of the season was about to start. It was a double green light start, and the two cars lurched forward at the same time. You could tell from the start, that it was gonna be a good one.

Just after they left the line, Tony began pulling away from Jess, and it looked bad. But halfway down the track Jess pulled up to dead even with him. Jess was beginning to sense that his suspicions were right. Tony got out in front, and just barely managed to stay there. He could have probably pulled way ahead if he wanted to but there was no need, he only had to lead by an inch.

Jess wished desperately that he had more to give, just enough to take Tony by an inch, but it wasn't happening. He was pushing the Sun-drop car for all it had, and he wasn't gaining on Tony at all. Just as he thought it might happen, something terrible happened.

PA-POW! Jess's motor gave a loud cough and cut out. There was a rapid loss of power, and the car began to slow. It was loud and Tony heard it. He also saw the yellow-painted nose of the Sun-drop car begin to fall back. He would be running dangerously close to his dial, and it looked like he had already won the race. In confidence, he let off his accelerator to come in with a good time.

Jess's heart sank. They came this close, went through all that trouble, even built a new motor right at the track--and now this.

"SHOOT! SHOOT! SHOOT!," Jess yelled out, and began stomping the pedal to the floor with every yell.

"SHOOT! SHOOOOOT!" He continued stomping. With the last stomp, a miracle happened. The motor regained power.

The car had lost about three-quarters of a car length to Tony by the time it regained power. The good thing is that it came back with a vengeance, with what felt like more acceleration than it had ever had before. He was coming up quick on the Trucker's car.

By the time Tony realized Jess coming up alongside him, it was too late. He stomped his gas and tried to regain his one-inch lead but the Sun-drop car had already built up enough momentum that he could not catch it.

Jess took the line first and the win light. They had identical reaction times, but Jess crossed first by .001 seconds. The whole crowd cheered for the underdog.

Jess cruised off the track and headed for the winner's circle. There was a big banner strung up behind the tower-side bleacher, where they were waiting to take his picture. The crew cheered and waved as he pulled up--along with plenty of fans and friends. Josie was there with her dad. Mr. Teague, Stanley, and many others from Teague's Beverage, came out to congratulate him as well. There were so many we had trouble squeezing in, but we finally got a chance to hug our sons and shake their hands.

Tony was having a bad time at his trailer. His dad was ranting and raving as he pulled Tony out of the car. He might have hit him if the sheriff's deputy hadn't been walking up.

The owner of the Logging-sponsored car that had lost to Jess with a red light, accompanied the deputy. They were interested in Zack's demon kart, mostly the engines. It looked like the whole Patterson bunch was going to have a bad evening.

In the winner's circle, Jess and the crew took many pictures. Some were for the track, some were for the paper, scrapbooks and so on. The business owners, who donated the charity money, had a picture made presenting the crew a big check. Afterwards, one of the businessmen approached them. It was Bay City's top veterinarian. He wanted to talk to them about Sloppy's condition and give them a proposal.

There was a big party thrown at Fred's in honor of the boys' victory. There was free pizza and Sun-drop for everyone. Everybody came, including Engine Joe. It was there last bash of the summer, and everyone made it a good one. Dancing, playing games, eating pizza, and reminiscing stories from the go-kart-filled summer.

Labor Day afternoon, they all got together one last time at the shop before the summer was over, and drove their go-karts down to Harvey's. He had gotten Sloppy back from the vet, and the two of them were sitting out under the awning. They managed to keep secret from him their reason for wanting to win so badly.

"So, how'd you boys do in da big race?" He asked.

"We won. It wasn't easy, but we won," Jess told him.

"Dat's good. So, what you gonna do wit all your prize money? Make some even faster go-karts?," He asked.

"No. I think we've got fast enough go-karts for a while. We something a little different in mind for the money."

The boys got out the check and told him their intentions. It was Sloppy and the old junkyard that had pushed them to the top. They wanted to thank him by paying for Sloppy's surgery. They also told him how the best vet in the area was willing to do the surgery for less than half price. That left enough money for the boys to buy materials to build Harvey a nice fence and clean up the yard near the trail. They planned to exhibit some of his old blacksmithing equipment outside the fence, with plaques describing their uses and impact on the history of industry. That way, Harvey's old junk really could be called an "Antique Décor."

The old German had tears rolling down his plump cheeks as the boys told him their intentions. Sloppy had been his best friend for many years. The rough-looking old dog was the only thing that had helped him get through the loss of his wife several years earlier. He was glad he was getting to keep his familiar old junk, and his best friend would no longer be in pain. Most of all, he was glad the boys cared so much, that they would work so hard for him.

▪▪

It was a beautiful fall day. When the bell rang at three, there was a mad dash out the double doors. Kids were scrambling everywhere. Jess was in the lead, with his former crewmembers close behind. They ran past where the bike racks used to be and climbed on their go-karts. They were in a hurry to get to Fred's for some pizza and Sun-drop.

ABOUT THE AUTHOR

Dennis Van Vleet grew up on two farms; one in Wisconsin and one in Texas. He made lifelong friends in both places who shared in experiencing the same kind of hijinks told in his stories. When he was eleven he wanted two things: a set of drums and a go-kart. He still has both and each has forever changed his life.